Hanging Day

Wrongly convicted of his wife's murder, Josh Tillman busts out of jail the night before he is due to hang. Rather than go on the run, he heads home determined to prove his innocence and track down his wife's killer. He has no evidence and no witnesses to back up his story. His father-in-law, cattle baron Stover Meckets, wants him dead and a corrupt prison guard is chasing him, determined to claim the price on his head.

A hanging posse has trailed him from the prison and is closing in. When the preacher who conducted his wedding ceremony turns up out of nowhere and has the nerve to stand up for Tillman, he is shot in cold blood.

With no one to help him, can Tillman figure out who the killer is and find enough evidence to prove it before the posse arrives and strings him up from a tree in his own backyard?

Hanging Day

Rob Hill

A Black Horse Western

ROBERT HALE · LONDON

© Hanging Day 2015
First published in Great Britain 2015

ISBN 978-0-7198-1532-4

Robert Hale Limited
Clerkenwell House
Clerkenwell Green
London EC1R 0HT

www.halebooks.com

Typeset by
Derek Doyle & Associates, Shaw Heath
Printed and bound in Great Britain by
CPI Antony Rowe, Chippenham and Eastbourne

1

Josh Tillman's heart hammered so hard he thought his ribs would crack. Lying on the narrow bench in his pitch-black cell, hardly daring to breathe, he counted every one of the guard's steps as he shuffled the length of the flag-stone passage. Eventually, the dispirited trudge came to a halt outside his door. An iron key clattered in the lock and the strangled shriek of the hinges echoed through the darkened jail.

Someone must have heard; everyone must have. It must have woken the whole place. The steel door inched open. Tillman's fingers dug into the sides of the bench. He waited for the sound of the uniform being thrown in. Each second was an age. Then it came, a collapsing sound like dust falling. Then there was another, harder this time, a leather slap against the stone flags: boots. Outside in the passage the footsteps began again. They retreated towards the desk where the duty guards played gin to kill time and waited for their shift to end.

Tillman sprang off the bench and felt for the clothes. He tore off his prison stripes and wrestled himself into the uniform. Too small. The pants were tight and he could only do up a couple of the buttons of the jacket. It would look ridiculous; everyone would know. He jammed his feet into the boots. His first step towards the door reminded him that this was the first time he had not been barefoot in a month.

At the same time as he felt for the edge of the open door, Tillman trod on something soft. Revulsion. Had some animal crawled into his cell and died in the darkness? Or had the guard lobbed in a rodent corpse with the clothes? Sometimes the guards threw dead rats into the cells at chow time and kept the prisoners' food for themselves. Then he realized. He reached down and felt for the cap which went with the uniform. If his heart hadn't been threatening to fracture his ribcage, he would have laughed.

The hinges screeched as Tillman prised open the door and slid into the corridor. The darkness was as thick as pitch. He froze. Out here, you could hear muffled shouts from behind the cell doors; men cried for mercy as their nightmares bore down on them. You could hear moans as they implored forgiveness in their dreams. It took a moment for Tillman's eyes to focus on the light. At the end of the corridor a stub of tallow made a yellow pool. There was a pile of cards beside the candle; the guards' chairs were empty. Tillman strained his eyes. If there was anyone in the shadows, he couldn't see them. He ran his hand down the edge of the door and found the lock. The key jutted out like a broken bone.

Easing the cell door closed, Tillman tried to muffle the screech of the hinges. When he turned the key, the snap of the lock ricocheted like a gunshot. He froze. His heartbeat galloped in his ears; a drop of sweat ran down his spine. He slid the key out of the lock and took his first steps towards the light.

Tillman checked his instinct to run, to get out of there fast. He forced his footsteps to imitate the guard's hopeless trudge. He stared ahead into the shadows around the pool of candlelight; he strained to hear a movement. He expected a trap. At any second someone could step forward and gun him down for sport. He waited for the snick of a hammer being ratcheted back.

But nothing happened. Tillman made himself concentrate so his footsteps didn't sound as though he was in a hurry. He reached the desk. No one launched themselves at him out of the darkness. No one cocked a weapon or fired a shot. There was just the sound of prisoners crying out in their sleep and the skitter of rats in the darkness.

The corridor angled here. A short passage led to the door on to the yard where the scaffold waited for him and the other wretches lying, moaning, in their cells. The door was open. In the sky above the prison walls Tillman saw the grey predawn wash of early day. Fear knifed through him. It was too light. His cell door was supposed to have been unlocked when night was thickest. The guard at the gate could recognize him. If the judge and his posse had arrived early for the hangings, they could be out there right now.

As he turned towards the door Tillman's heart skipped. So far the plan was working. There would be a horse waiting for him outside. All he had to do was ride straight up to the main gate, where the duty guard would believe he was just a guy from the night shift who had decided to sneak off early. Nothing unusual: they all did it. Just had to be careful not to catch the guard's eye, to keep his face turned to the shadows. His steps slowed as he approached the open door. One step outside, he dropped back into the doorway.

The yard was empty. The gallows reared above the prison wall, silhouetted against a cobalt sky. For the past three days, from his cell window, Tillman had watched the carpenters work. He listened to the trap slam open as they tested the drop and watched the sandbag pirouette mockingly at the end of the rope. When they caught sight of him behind the bars they called out, boasted how good their craftsmanship was, laughed as they told him he should be grateful to them because his neck would snap like a twig.

The rectangular yard was surrounded by a twenty-four-foot adobe wall. The cell block ran along one side. At the far end, the guards' bunkhouse and mess room stood next to the stables; at the opposite end was the main gate and the viewing platforms reached by ladders, which the guards used when prisoners were let out for exercise. Tillman could just make out the shape of the cottonwood guardhouse beside the gate. Some sentry would be asleep in there. He would have to wake him.

Tillman took a step into the yard, felt the cool night breeze against his face and turned to the hitching rail beside the door. No horse. His nerves splintered; his knees jellied under him. The horse was supposed to be right here. That was the agreement; that was the plan. That was what he had promised to pay for. He fought to stop his thoughts spiralling away in panic. Maybe the horse was tethered somewhere else. He scanned the shadows. The rail next to the gate was empty; no horse was tethered outside the stable.

Tillman's brain cartwheeled. Even if he made it across the yard and through the gate, there was a hundred miles of desert between here and the nearest town. Without a horse, without a canteen of water and with the guards on his tail he would be dead by noon. Was this a trick? There were rumours of guards who allowed prisoners to escape in the night and then picked them off with Sharps rifles as dawn rose. No one knew if they did it to claim a reward or just for sport. No escaper had ever got further than a couple of miles. Tillman glanced back at the gallows. Hanging above the trap, the noose watched him like an empty eye. What choice did he have? At sunup he was dead anyway.

He stepped out from the shadows and headed straight across the yard towards the gate. Forcing himself to keep to the same weary pace he had used when he left the cell, he stayed away from the shadows that clung to the walls of the building. Out in the open, he told himself, it looked as though he had nothing to hide.

Halfway across the yard, nothing stirred. If anyone was watching from the cell block they kept quiet. If a guard could see him from the guardhouse there was no sign. Tillman pulled his cap down, stared at the ground and kept up the same shuffling pace. Two steps away from the guardhouse door, still nothing. Should he knock or walk straight in? He was just making up his mind to say that he had orders to make sure the gate was open ready for the judge's arrival, when the door swung wide and two men in guards' uniforms stepped out. Each of them held a Winchester levelled at his belly.

Tillman stopped dead, raised his hands slowly and stared at them. He recognized one of the guards. It was Tommy Ludza, a sharp-faced guy with broken veins on his cheeks and a thatch of greasy blond hair. His body was thin, his movements were quick and his eyes were cold. In addition to the regulation Winchester he always carried a Bowie in his belt, casually shoved at an angle behind the buckle. The prisoners loathed him. He was always trying to hustle Bull Durham or offering to smuggle in contraband red-eye for an outrageous price. No one trusted him further than they could spit, but when Tillman decided to break for freedom and needed to bribe a guard, Tommy Ludza was the obvious choice.

Tillman's problem was that he had nothing to bribe Ludza with. He needed a horse, someone to let him out of his cell and someone to open the main gate. He promised Ludza the $300 that he kept buried at the back of his cabin. He knew Ludza's illicit transactions never amounted to more than a buck or two at a time, so $300 would be a fortune to him. Knowing that the date for Tillman's execution was approaching, Ludza stalled, pretended he couldn't make up his mind whether he could trust Tillman and all the time tried to push the price up. Tillman refused to budge. He was offering $300. It was all he had.

The previous day Ludza caved in. He arranged to take the night shift. He promised he would unlock Tillman's cell, provide a guard's uniform, leave the cell-block door open and tether a horse outside. He said he would wait outside the main gate, so together they would ride to Tillman's place, where Tillman would hand over the money. Ludza would then high-tail it back to the jail in time to pick up his shift the following day, by which time Tillman would be on his way.

Tillman calculated that once they were outside the jail walls there was a good chance Ludza would shoot him, drag his body back and try to talk his way into some kind of reward. If they got as far as the money Ludza would want to kill him anyway. Right now, staring down the barrels of the two Winchesters, none of this mattered.

Tillman had gambled on Ludza's greed but had underestimated the extent of it.

Ludza waved his rifle to indicate Tillman should step into the guardhouse. The second guard followed behind him and jabbed the barrel of his Winchester into Tillman's kidneys. Inside the cottonwood building the air smelled of sweat and tobacco. There was a table with an unlit oil lamp and a couple of benches pushed casually aside. It was as dark as the cell Tillman had just left.

'Key?' Ludza's voice rasped like a cat spitting.

Tillman handed over his cell key and watched as Ludza threaded it back on to the steel hoop attached to his belt.

'Change of plan,' Ludza went on. 'We're gonna kill you now.'

His thin lips angled into a smile. Tillman heard the second guard pull back the hammer on his Winchester.

'Or you can give us six hundred.'

The Winchester barrel rammed into his kidneys again.

'Three hundred,' Tillman said. 'We agreed.'

'You know what's gonna happen come sunup,' Ludza said.

'Three hundred,' Tillman said. His voice could have hammered in nails.

He caught his breath as the Winchester drove into his kidneys.

'If we shoot you right now,' Ludza leaned towards him until Tillman could feel his breath on his face, 'we get a reward. No problem.'

'You're lying,' Tillman gasped. The pain made it difficult to breathe. 'You shoot me now, they'll put you on half pay for letting me out of the cell.'

He swung his arm behind him and knocked the Winchester barrel aside. Ludza shoved his rifle into

11

Tillman's chest.

'Don't you try nothing.'

The smile still angled Ludza's mouth, but his eyes blazed.

'Three hundred,' Tillman said. 'We're wasting time.'

'Horses ain't here,' Ludza said. 'They're locked in the stable and I ain't got a key.'

Tillman's belly turned to water. He turned to look out through the guardroom door. In the east, pale morning light crept into the sky.

Ignoring the rifles, Tillman grabbed a fistful of Ludza's uniform.

'We had a deal.'

Tillman shook him, practically lifting him off the ground.

The second guard slipped his rifle across Tillman's neck, jammed his knee into the small of Tillman's back and yanked his head back to cut off his air. Tillman dropped Ludza, watched him stagger back a few paces and brush down the front of his uniform.

'Let him go,' Ludza snapped.

The guard moved his rifle away. Tillman doubled over, gulped mouthfuls of air while his hands tried to ease the pain in his throat.

'You listen to me.' Ludza's voice was steel. 'The guy with the horses ain't showed, that's all.'

His weasel words echoed in Tillman's head. He was trying to convince Tillman of something, trying to cut some deal. For a moment Tillman hardly listened. All he could think was that there was light in the sky.

'Open the gate,' Tillman said. His throat burned and made it difficult to get the words out. 'Let me out.'

'Think you'll make it?' Ludza laughed. 'Soon as they

find your cell empty they'll be laying odds as to which one is going to put a bullet in you first.'

'Give me a rifle and let me go,' Tillman said. 'When you catch up with me, I'll have the money ready.'

The smile sloped Ludza's mouth again like a pencil mark.

'Think I'm stupid? We wait here until Judge Duval comes. He'll have his posse with him to see the hangings. You take one of their horses like you're going to lead it to the stable. Instead of that, you head for the gate. . . .'

Tillman made a dive for Ludza again but his rifle was levelled at his chest.

'Why didn't you get me a horse? If the judge sees me I'm a dead man.'

'Horses cost money.' Ludza shrugged. 'Three hundred ain't enough.'

He studied Tillman's face, looked for some movement in the mouth or some shadow in the eyes that meant Tillman would weaken.

'I ain't got time for this,' the second guard said suddenly. 'I got to watch the gate. Judge will be here soon. He don't like to be kept waiting.'

Tillman turned to look at the sky again.

'Get him out of here.' The guard sounded nervous. 'You ain't going to get another three hundred out of him. Best lock him back up in his cell and if he won't go, shoot him in the head. Either way, I don't want to know. I ain't seen nothing.'

With his Winchester under his arm the guard left the wooden guardhouse and crossed the yard to the main gate. He opened a flap which let him spy on the world outside and stood with his face pressed against a grille.

Ludza stepped back from Tillman and sat down on one

13

of the benches. He kept his rifle steady and trained on Tillman's gut.

'He gets nervous whenever the judge's due,' Ludza explained. 'I think he's wrong about another three hundred though. I think you're good for it.'

Tillman watched the smile slip its way along Ludza's mouth again.

'See, I trust you,' Ludza went on. 'I've already paid five bucks to the guy who should have been on the night shift with me to stay away sick. Promised I'd do a shift for him next week as well.'

'So what?' Tillman said.

Ludza's face hardened.

'You sure you remembered to lock your cell door?'

Tillman nodded.

'That will buy us some time,' Ludza said. 'I'm going to say one of the prisoners escaped. I'll say I don't know which one. I'll say he knifed one of the guards.'

'What?' Tillman didn't follow.

'How do you think you're going to get past this guy without paying him off?' Ludza nodded towards the guard keeping watch for the judge. He was telling Tillman something but Tillman couldn't properly grasp what it was.

'You ain't giving him a share of the three hundred?'

Ludza's mouth tightened.

'Hell I am. You've seen what he's like; you think he ain't gonna squawk the minute the judge asks him a question?'

He gestured with the rifle.

'I'll fetch a couple of horses from the stable. Soon as the gate's open, make a run for it. I'll be right behind you. There'll be others following. I'll have to tell 'em or they'll know it was me let you out. If they catch up with us I'll have to shoot you.' Ludza paused. 'There'll be a reward for bringing back a prisoner who knifed a guard.'

'Knifed a guard?' Tillman still didn't understand.

'Wait here,' Ludza snapped.

Winchester in his hand, he strode out of the guard-room. Tillman watched him march the length of the yard to the stable and use his Bowie to jemmy the lock. He kicked the door open and a few minutes later led out two appaloosas. Next he crossed to the guards' bunkhouse and hammered on the door with his rifle butt.

'Prisoner escaped!' he yelled.

By this time the guard keeping watch had turned from the gate and was staring open-mouthed at Ludza, who led the ponies towards him.

'Hey, Tommy, what's going on?'

'Prisoner escaped,' Ludza said calmly. 'Open the gate. I'm going after him.'

'I didn't see nothing.' The guard sounded rattled; he knew he could wind up in trouble for this. He drew back the heavy bolts and started to heave open the gate.

'Going after him on your own?' The guard stared at Ludza, incredulous. 'These guys are as dangerous as snakes.'

'This one is,' Ludza said. 'He knifed a guard.'

'Who was it?' The tremble returned to the guard's voice.

There were shouts from the guardhouse at the far end of the yard, the stamp of feet on a wooden floor.

Ludza slipped the Bowie from his belt and jabbed the broad blade upwards between the guard's ribs. He held the knife there for a second, pulled it free and watched the man slump to the ground at his feet; dark blood blossomed across the front of his uniform.

'You, you fool.'

Tillman had already mounted up. As Ludza swung himself up into the saddle of one of the appaloosas Tillman careered past him, through the open gate and out into the empty desert.

2

Tillman turned his pony south and rode hard. There had been no rain for months; the desert floor was bedrock and the going was fast. There were no tracks in this direction, just miles of flat, dry land, beavertail and yucca. As the sky lightened the saguaro flowers closed tight as fists to defend themselves against the day. Families of jack rabbits watched him pass; a group of cactus wrens bathing in the dirt stopped and eyed him; a blackthroat lighted on the branch of an ironwood bush and turned, momentarily curious.

Way out in the flats, Tillman reined in the pony. His shoulders ached from holding his position in the saddle; the cool air chilled his skin and cold had entered his bones. He cast his eye back the way he had come. No one. No search party. Not even Ludza. Just the wide, empty land, the red desert floor and the black outlines of the cactus plants etched against the breaking day.

Miles back, the prison building squatted in the landscape like a sickly toad. The adobe roofs and walls were dung coloured; the gates gleamed like the retina of a blind eye. Tillman stared at the route he had taken. Where was Ludza? It was impossible that no one was chasing him.

17

Dawn had broken so, by rights, he should be a dead man.

The judge would have reached the jail by now. Had he decided to leave Tillman to the vultures? Maybe he thought it wasn't worth risking the lives of his posse to chase one condemned man.

Tillman's thoughts hurtled one after another. Was it possible the judge had tumbled to Ludza's part in all this? Maybe someone had seen him knife the guard. Maybe they had slung him in a cell. Maybe he had confessed. Maybe the judge had declared himself jury and executioner and Ludza was swinging from the gibbet right now. Tillman shielded his eyes with the flat of his hand and examined the landscape for the giveaway dust cloud that would show that a rider was on his trail.

In the east, the grey dawn had softened into a wash of glaucous blue. A layer of rose-coloured cloud rested above it, and below, a thread of gold stretched the length of the horizon. Like a shard of bone, the sliver of a crescent moon still hung in the sky. Ahead lay more miles of empty flats; far beyond, black granite mountains reared against the early sky. Tillman leaned down and patted the neck of his pony. The animal turned her head, nickered and shook her mane to indicate willingness to press on. Tillman clicked his tongue and nudged with his heels. Concerned to rest her after the flat-out gallop, he walked her forward.

In a few hours, heat would bludgeon down. There was no shade and the only water he had was what was contained in the canteen Ludza had tied to the saddle. It didn't matter. Nothing mattered apart from getting back home to find the evidence which proved he was an innocent man. The thought buzzed in Tillman's brain like flies: what evidence? So far as he knew, there wasn't any.

18

Everyone back at the ranch believed he was guilty, or said they did. Stover Meckets, ranch owner, Tillman's father-in-law and old friend, was convinced; he was the one who had called the sheriff. Harlan, Meckets' young nephew, swore blind it was Tillman who had killed June. Frank Whipple's son, Joe, the only other person on the ranch at the time, backed them up.

The minute the judge passed sentence, Tillman made up his mind to petition the Governor. When his appeal was turned down flat he knew he had to bust out of jail. Weeks ago, in the corner of the prison yard, he had offered Ludza a bribe.

'Telling me you're innocent?' Ludza laughed.

Heads bowed, eyes screwed up against the vicious sunlight, the condemned men shuffled round the perimeter, trying to keep tight to the shade of the walls.

'You and everyone else in here.' Ludza smirked. 'So what? You're all going to hang anyway.'

'Three hundred,' Tillman said. 'I got it hidden.'

'You got three hundred dollars?' Ludza sneered. 'You're lying. You think you can get round me like that?'

But Tillman knew he had taken the bait. There was a hesitation in Ludza's voice when he mentioned the money; his contempt was a touch too quick when it curled off his tongue. Tillman decided to leave it a couple of days before he tried again.

The problem was, there was no set routine for the condemned prisoners. They got fed when the guards felt like it or could be bothered or remembered. Two weeks could pass before they were allowed out of their stinking cells into the exercise yard. Then they could be allowed out three days running. Other days, they were sent straight back to their cells before they had time to walk a single circuit. Tillman couldn't say when he would see Ludza again.

He needn't have worried. Ludza came to him.

One night, instead of pushing the bowl of slop through the flap at the bottom of the cell door, Tillman heard the iron key bang into the lock as Ludza let himself in. He slid the bowl across the floor to Tillman with his foot while he covered him with his rifle.

'OK, Mr Innocent. What you got for me?'

A thin smile sloped across his face.

'They got me sentenced to hang for murder.' Tillman hesitated. 'I never killed nobody.' He fought to keep his voice matter-of-fact. 'I've got to get out and clear my name.'

'Somebody frame you as well?' A mocking laugh scratched Ludza's throat. 'Like I said, this whole jail's full of innocent men.'

'Three hundred if you help me,' Tillman said. 'If not, I ask somebody else.'

'You don't say nothing to no one.' Ludza waved his rifle dangerously. 'I'll get you out of here but I want six.'

Tillman stared at the cell floor. Suddenly nothing seemed so bad. The tiny high window let in more light; the stone floor felt warm under his bare feet; the thick walls were almost comforting. He had hooked Ludza; now all he had to do was reel him in.

'Still a few weeks till they slip that noose round your neck.' Ludza's smirk pencilled across his mouth. 'That's enough time for you to come up with another three hundred.'

Tillman didn't answer.

'Who is it you're supposed to have killed anyhow?'

Tillman looked at him. Rifle or no rifle, he gripped the

edge of the bench to stop himself from lashing out. In that moment, what he wanted most in the world was to plant his fist in the middle of Ludza's leering face.

'I said who was it you killed?' Ludza paused. 'Or didn't kill.' He corrected himself a shade too deliberately.

But Tillman had himself under control now. He answered straight.

'They said I shot my wife.'

There was no expression in his voice, no emotion, just a statement of cold fact.

'Put a bullet in your old lady?' Ludza laughed. 'Wouldn't be the first who wanted to do that.'

Tillman stared calmly at him. He rested his hands on the edge of the bench.

'You want the three hundred, you'll get me out of here. And you'll never mention her again.'

Ludza jabbed the rifle barrel into Tillman's chest.

'Six hundred.' His eyes blazed. 'Or one fine morning they're gonna haul you out of here, put a bag over your head and a rope round your neck. And that's the last thing you're gonna know.'

The air was warm on Tillman's face now. The sun had climbed above the horizon. In the far distance, the granite peaks turned purple in the morning light. The desert floor was sandy here; shin daggers and saguaro had given way to velvet mesquite and creosote scrub. Patches of bright verbena caught the light. Tillman looked back. Still no one was following.

The pony picked up speed at the touch of Tillman's heels. By the time the day was hottest, Tillman judged he would be in the centre of the flats, midway between the jail and the mountains. By sundown he would be in the foothills; if anyone was following him he could be sure of losing them by then. After dark he could turn west and make the wide arc for home.

This far out into the desert the only sound was the regular thud of the pony's hoofs. Not yet nine in the morning and already the heat bounced off the sand. Tillman undid the buttons of his uniform jacket and fell to musing on his escape. The original idea had been that he and Ludza would ride out of the jail together: two guards coming off duty. So far, nothing Ludza had decided on had gone according to plan. Tillman guessed the guard in charge of the livery demanded a bribe for leaving the door unlocked and Ludza refused to pay.

With any luck, Tillman reflected, he would never see Ludza again. But if he was caught and Ludza was still around, Ludza would pin the blame on him for knifing the guard at the gate. Despite the warm air Tillman shuddered. He remembered the expression of horrified surprise on the man's face, his uniform drenched in blood and the way the appaloosa almost trampled his dying body.

With the heat of the day building, Tillman decided to rest his pony and walk. He climbed down from the saddle and patted the appaloosa's neck. In return, the animal nudged his shoulder. After another hour, the air melted like glass. Sometimes the mountains reared right in front of him; a minute later they danced so far away Tillman thought he had covered no distance at all. Dizzy with the heat and with sweat stinging his eyes, he caught his foot in a rabbit hole, missed his footing and stumbled. As the burning air truncheoned the back of his neck he pulled off his jacket and hauled it over his head and shoulders. His pace slowed to a crawl.

*

Tillman lost track of time. The sun blinded him; the desert sand burned through the soles of his boots; against his face, the air felt like he was standing next to a stove. He hung his head and relied on the frail protection of his cotton jacket.

Tillman had carried the taste of sand in his mouth for hours. Back at the jail, when he first set eyes on the canteen tied to the saddle, he had made a deal with himself that he wouldn't take a sip until midday. Now, if he dared glance up at the sun, the light stabbed his eyes and made his head ring. It had to be time.

But as soon as he held the canteen in his hand, he knew. He wrestled off the cap, tipped it up at his lips and jerked his head back so that the jacket dropped behind him. A line of sand trickled into his open mouth and made him retch. Tillman gripped the edge of his saddle until his knuckles cracked. He fought down the fury that reared inside him. He mustn't use up his energy with anger; he mustn't waste it on despair.

Hawking out the dirt from his dry mouth, Tillman flung the canteen aside and reached down to grab his jacket. The sun punched down and bruised his uncovered skull. He was dizzy, all the strength went out of him; he thought he might fall. He jammed his foot in the stirrup, heaved himself up and let the appaloosa take him where it would.

For the next hours Tillman was almost dreaming. Faintly aware of the plodding steps of the pony beneath him, he took comfort from the even pace. Heat branded the back of his head and scourged his shoulders. With the reins curled round his wrist, the concussing heat dragged him to the edge of consciousness. He had to fight to stay awake.

By now, Tillman didn't care about Ludza or whatever double-cross he had been working on. He was away from the prison and, by some fluke of good fortune, nobody was following him. If he got to the mountains, he would be safe. He would have a view over the whole plain; he could pick up a trail and nobody would know where he was.

Through the burning thirst and pounding heat, one thought kept Tillman going: he had to clear his name. He had to find Meckets, his one-time friend and partner and convince him. He had to find out who the real killer was.

Fresh from Texas, when Tillman had first met him, Meckets came over as a tough cattleman on the make. After consumption took his wife he was determined to make a new start for himself and June, his eighteen-year-old daughter. He brought along his young nephew, Harlan, collected his beeves together and drove them west in search of virgin land. He knew Texas cattlemen were making fortunes; he had heard stories about Chisum and Goodnight, their vast herds and long drives. Why shouldn't he do the same in Arizona? Given a few years, he was determined to be as rich as them. He planned to team up with someone who knew the country, stake a claim and build a herd.

Tillman had been drifting through the territory for a year when Meckets ran into him. Like Meckets, he too was looking for a place to settle down but, without cash or capital, had ended up moving from farm to ranch, settling for odd jobs or carpentry work in the towns that sprang up. Arizona Territory was wide open then. Since the Apaches had run off the Mexicans and the white men had run off the Apaches, land was there for the taking. Anyone with grit and ambition could lay claim to hundreds of square miles.

Tillman brought Meckets to a wide, south-facing valley protected by two shoulders of rising land in the foothills of a chain of unforgiving granite peaks. It narrowed to a creek at the south end. Winter precipitation on the high ground fed the stream which ran the length of the valley which meant there was grazing all year. Squirrel tail and tangle head grass carpeted the slopes; ferns clung to fissures in the outcrops of rock. On the valley floor, milkweed, blood flowers, marigold and horsemint decorated the banks of the stream. Added to this, there was enough lumber on the high land to build cabins and, with careful management, enough topsoil lower down to grow sweet corn and cantaloupes, maybe even lettuce and potatoes. Meckets named the place Eden and staked his claim.

But Meckets wasn't the only emigrant from the Lone Star state. At that time many ranchers moved West; some of them brought longhorns with them as the basis of new breeding herds. The problem was that when the ranchers moved, rustlers moved with them. Boundaries were insecure or non-existent; distances were so vast, no one could tell where one spread ended and the neighbour's began; hands were hired locally and were new to the job. The rustlers had a field day.

Meckets trusted Tillman. He knew at once he was the kind of guy he was looking for and offered to make him a partner straight off. Tillman was hard-working, reliable, honest and good with a gun. He didn't have much of a head for business but he was even-tempered and would get on well with the hired men. He could take decisions, and if he had to spend days and nights out on the range on his own it wouldn't bother him. He had an impressive talent for drawing too, which was something Meckets had never come across before. Tillman used to come back from a few days out with the herd with a full sketch book: landscapes, portraits of cattle and accurate pencil drawings of the local flora. Meckets talked about making frames for the sketches of his prize breeding stock and hanging them in pride of place.

Although it took Tillman a while to figure out why, Harlan didn't take to him. Having to share his uncle's attention made Harlan jealous. In addition, when Meckets offered Tillman a partnership Harlan had the feeling that something was being given away which was rightfully his. Also, although he had jumped at the chance of riding with his uncle from Texas to set up a ranch in uncharted Arizona, the novelty soon wore off. The life was lonely and the work was hard; at nineteen years old he craved company and excitement. Although he was nominally a partner in the operation, Meckets didn't trust him to handle money. Instead, he paid him a wage, which Harlan promptly blew at poker tables whenever he could find a saloon. This led to rows and resentment on both sides.

The one thing that kept Harlan interested in the ranch was June. They were the same age. Harlan tried to impress her in all the wrong ways. Boastful about his shooting, he made her watch as he lined up tin cans on a fence; exaggerating his skills with a lasso, he insisted she stand by the corral as he flung his rope after a bull calf; he hiked up stories about how well he handled his liquor and lied about how much he won at cards. At first, she didn't grasp that all this boasting was a peacock display designed to impress her.

In the second year they were in Arizona June was alarmed when Harlan plucked up the courage to announce he was sweet on her. She tried laughing it off,

26

but he was insistent; she told him they were cousins but he said it didn't matter. By this time, she had begun to enjoy Tillman's company. She had been out for walks along the stream with him and she loved it when he let her see his sketches of the ranch. Although she didn't realize it, Harlan noticed. Resentment burned inside him like a fuse.

While June was patient and forgiving with Harlan, Meckets grew exasperated and angry.

In one furious row about Harlan's gambling losses, Meckets refused to give him any more money. He even told his nephew Tillman was all the things he hoped young Harlan would turn out to be but plainly wasn't. Harlan was stung; his attitude to Meckets and the others changed. He swore that next time he went to Tucson he would use his share of the ranch as an IOU at the poker tables. He spent all his time with the hard-bitten guys in the bunkhouse; he cut Tillman dead, barely spoke to his uncle and avoided June.

Soon after that, the rustling problem got bad. The herd was cut time after time. Fifty head here, a hundred there. Sometimes as many as 200 head would be spirited through the narrows at the south end of the valley in a single night. Meckets suggested a good name for the place would be Stealer's Creek; Tillman agreed.

Meckets decided he needed a stock detective, someone who was self-reliant enough to spend days alone on the range, someone who was honest and had a sure sense of right and wrong and someone who wasn't afraid to use his gun. Tillman was the obvious candidate. But when Meckets suggested he take on the job, Tillman surprised him by turning it down, saying he wanted to spend more time around the ranch. Meckets soon discovered why.

Two other things happened that year, both of which changed life at the ranch for ever. The first was that Tillman asked June to marry him and she accepted. Although Meckets went along with it, he had secretly hoped that, when the time came, June would get hitched to the owner of one of the neighbouring ranches and that way an empire would be created. But he recognized that that was just wishful thinking. He liked Tillman; he knew he would treat June well. Meckets even had half an idea that he might find a way to cut Harlan out of the partnership at some time in the future, but he didn't have to worry about that now. In the fullness of time June might even produce a grandson who would inherit the ranch and Meckets' legacy would be secure.

The second thing that happened was a tragic accident, which shook the foundations of the place. Tillman shot and killed one of the hands. Frank Whipple was a hard drinker and bunkhouse cynic. He had been around ranches all his life and never tired of telling everyone he had nothing to show for it. His wife ran off with an itinerant garment salesman who had passed through back in the fall, and left him with their sixteen-year-old son, Joe, who idolized his father. With no wife and mother to cook for them, father and son moved into the bunkhouse with the men.

The rustling was at a high point. Meckets ordered the livery stable doors to be padlocked at the end of each day in case the thieves turned their attention to the horses. One tar black night, when the sky was moonless, Tillman heard someone breaking in. The sound of the hasp being levered off was unmistakable.

Tillman sprinted down to the stable door and called out three times for whoever it was to stop what he was doing. The man ignored him and carried on. Then Tillman heard a movement in the shadows, which meant that the man had an accomplice. He called one more time and when the man told him to go to hell, he fired.

The next thing that happened was that Meckets came careering down from the ranch house and in the light from his blazing torch they saw Frank Whipple lying dead. Standing beside him was Joe.

Tillman lurched in the saddle as the pony's hoofs slipped. Stony ground. He grabbed the jacket off his head. He had reached the edge of the foothills. Dry gullies cut by long-forgotton flash floods zigzagged down to the desert floor. Creosote scrub and silverbeard littered the slopes. Higher up, palo verde and eucalyptus spread their branches. More than that, even though the air shimmered, the brutal edge had gone out of the heat. Tillman slid down from the saddle and, half leaning against the pony, began to trudge up towards the trees.

A few yards further on Tillman almost blundered into a barrel cactus. It was eight feet high and as wide as the body of a man. The orange spines were fierce, but he managed to kick it over. He looked around for a sharp stone, anything with an edge which would allow him to slice off the top. The pony stood patiently and waited while he scoured the ground.

Eventually, Tillman had his hand inside the cactus and was scooping out the pulp. He shoved a handful into his mouth and chewed greedily. To his parched throat and swollen tongue it was nectar. He spat it out and started on another handful, squeezing droplets of moisture and feeling them run luxuriously down his throat. Then he was able to cup a handful of green liquid from the centre of

29

the cactus and lap it from his palm like a cat. The taste was acrid, but the few drops soothed him like balm.

Back along the way Tillman had come the air twisted and curled in the heat. The prison building was long out of view. Once he got higher, he thought, he would be able to find water, even if he had to dig to uncover a spring.

Tillman didn't hear the footstep behind him, but someone lobbed a canteen over his shoulder so it landed at his feet with a heavy thud. It was full. Tillman didn't have time to reach for it; he didn't have time to turn round. He felt the end of a cold rifle barrel jab into his neck and heard the snick of the hammer of a Winchester being pulled back.

A voice hissed in his ear.

'Six hundred, Tillman. Not a cent less.'

3

While the sun had dropped low enough to cast stubs of shadows, the air still buckled over the hot ground. Except for the chirp of cicadas in the junipers higher up the ridge, there was no sound. Tillman sat still, not turning to look.

'Didn't have to tell the judge you knifed that guard.' Ludza drove the steel tip of the Winchester barrel into Tillman's neck. 'He figured it for himself. Told him I saw you in your cell before I came off shift. Said one of the other guards must have slipped you a key; I showed him mine. If he looks hard enough, he might find the spare is missing from the guardhouse.'

Tillman ignored the laugh that tore at Ludza's throat, instead he watched the air twist. Far in the distance a redtail circled on the thermals; the bird had spotted his prey and was judging the time to swoop.

'Judge says hanging's too good for a guy like you,' Ludza said. 'He ain't a forgiving man.'

'You gonna let me have a drink?' Tillman said.

He palmed the Winchester barrel away from his neck, leaned forward and grabbed the canteen. He drank too fast. Water spilled down his throat and over his chin.

Washing away the dust in his mouth and the taste of cactus pith from his tongue, each sweet mouthful made him catch his breath.

'When a man gets convicted of murder, judge reckons he don't deserve no favours.'

Ludza had made up his mind to torment Tillman; he relished the opportunity for mockery.

'You should be grateful to me.'

Tillman screwed the cap back on the canteen. Let Ludza say what he liked, the feeling the cool water left in his throat was luxury.

'Freed you from jail,' Ludza said. 'Saved your life; brought you water in the desert; put myself in danger, all for a lousy three hundred.'

Tillman concentrated on the sensation the water had left in his throat.

'That's why three hundred ain't good enough.'

Ludza's voice jabbed at him like the barrel of the rifle.

'Could shoot you now,' he said. 'Judge might even make me a captain. No more night duties. No more standing round on platforms in the heat of the day.'

'Let's get going.' Tillman wasn't listening. 'Walk along the ridge for a couple of hours to rest the horses, then head west. We'll be at my place by midnight.'

'You thought you was going to slip away from me, coming out here,' Ludza kept on. 'That's what you were thinking, ain't it?'

'Never thought that,' Tillman said. 'I was surprised you weren't right behind me.'

Ludza laughed. 'Never occurred to you I'd take the long route and double back?'

Tillman got to his feet. He looked round at Ludza for the first time. The dirt-stained jacket of his uniform hung on his thin shoulders like a rag. Sand stuck to the sweat on his face and his mouth carried his usual insulting smile. He held the Winchester level with Tillman's belly.

'Go on ahead,' Ludza said. 'I'm right behind you this time.'

'Put your rifle down,' Tillman said. 'You slip on a rock and I could take a slug in the back.'

'Move.' Ludza gestured with the barrel of the gun. 'Lucky you ain't had a slug in the back already.'

Leading the appaloosa by the bridle, Tillman picked his way through a sea of jojoba bushes. Ludza kept a few paces behind. When Tillman glanced back, he saw that Ludza had shoved his rifle back in the saddle holster. Although the sun was still high and the air was warm, the brutal heat of the day had passed and made the climb easier that he had expected.

When Tillman looked round again Ludza had stopped to rummage through the grey jojoba leaves and fill his pockets with goat nuts.

'Stop you being hungry for a while,' he said. 'Ain't gonna get nothing else to eat.'

'How come you ain't with a search party?' Tillman said. He reached into the leathery leaves and found some nuts for himself.

'Told the judge my pa was sick.' The same thin smile slid across his mouth. 'Told him you'd said you'd head north if you ever broke out. That's the direction he's taken. Thanked me for raising the alarm and told me to catch up with them tomorrow.'

The goat nuts were soft-skinned and the flesh was easy to chew. As Tillman led the way along the side of the ridge, the woody taste reminded Tillman how hungry he was. At dusk, he turned west and picked up a deer trail. The further the temperature fell, the easier the going became. He mounted up again and, rested by the hours Tillman had led her, the appaloosa felt strong.

Although Ludza rode close behind Tillman, neither man spoke. Lack of food combined with fatigue from the hard day affected both of them. As the hours passed they were barely able to sit upright. They slumped forward in their saddles, shoulders hunched, heads lowered. Time after time they slipped into sleep, only to jolt themselves awake just as they were about to pitch headlong.

Shortly before midnight, with starlight washing over everything, Tillman led them up a slope into the neatly kept yard of a single-storey cabin. It had a stone chimney at one end and a low-roofed porch along the wall facing the yard. The window shutters were fastened back as though someone had left in a hurry and forgot to close the place up. A well stood in the centre of the yard with a rusty cattle trough beside it. Along the boundary, opposite the house, a line of junipers had been planted for shade and beyond them was a view over Eden Valley.

'Nice place,' Ludza said. 'Yours?'

Tillman levered himself out of the saddle and headed over to the well. He dropped the bucket and filled the trough for the horses.

'Where's the money?' Ludza said.

He pulled the Winchester out of its saddle holster before he made to dismount.

'Buried out back,' Tillman said. 'Best get a couple of hours shuteye. I'll do the digging at first light.'

'Think I've rode all this way so you can go to sleep?' Ludza ratcheted the lever on the Winchester. 'Find your-self a shovel.'

Tillman tethered the horses to one of the junipers and

led the way round the back of the cabin where a lean-to was covered over by a piece of canvas. He pulled back the cover to reveal a collection of shovels, picks and saws, all cleaned and neatly stacked.

Ludza watched Tillman walk to the end of the cabin wall, stand still for a moment, then count ten deliberate strides at a right angle to the building. When he stopped, he swung his pick. Winchester across his knees, Ludza sank down with his back against the wall and watched.

Inside half an hour there was a hole deep enough for Tillman to climb into. As soon as his spade hit metal he threw it down, reached in and lifted out a tin box. Inside were two packages wrapped in oilcloth, each tied with a leather lace. Ludza scrambled to his feet.

'I want six hundred,' Ludza said. 'But I'll take everything you've got.'

'Did you tell the judge where this place was?' Tillman said.

'Didn't have to. He makes a point of knowing all about the guys he plans to hang.' Ludza smirked. 'Guess it makes it feel personal.'

Tillman pulled at the ties round one of the packages.

'Is that the money?' Ludza snapped. He waved the Winchester dangerously.

Tillman lobbed the second package over to him.

'Sure is.'

With the rifle in his hands, Ludza missed the catch. In the moment he stooped to retrieve it, Tillman was on his feet, a .45 in his hand. The oilcloth wrapper lay on the ground.

But Ludza saw. When his shot from the Winchester went wide, he hurled himself at Tillman and skittled his legs out from under him. Tillman's shot ricocheted off the cabin roof as he pitched over backwards. Tillman was alarmed to discover how weeks of jailhouse gruel had leached his strength.

With a swing of the rifle butt Ludza clubbed the .45 out of Tillman's hand and sent it spinning into the darkness. Tillman couldn't hold him off. Ludza jammed the Winchester crossways down on to his throat. Seizing the rifle with both hands, with one almighty heave, Tillman managed to shove Ludza aside long enough to scramble out from underneath the gun. While Ludza fumbled with the lever of the Winchester and swung the barrel, Tillman jumped to his feet.

By the time Ludza loosed off a shot Tillman had hurled himself round the side of the cabin. The slug bit into the wooden wall. Tillman launched himself across the yard and into the junipers. His heart smashing behind his ribs, he ducked down between the trees and waited for Ludza to sneak into view.

A second later the barrel of the Winchester nosed round the corner of the cabin. Keeping back in the shadows, Ludza peered cautiously to left and right into the yard. At one point he stared directly at the brush that shielded Tillman. For a second Tillman was convinced he was about to level the Winchester and take a shot. Instead, he called out:

'No need for this, Tillman.'

He sounded plausible, friendly even. Tillman watched as he edged the Winchester up to his shoulder and swung the barrel in an arc to cover the line of trees. Tillman didn't answer.

'Why don't you come on out?' Ludza couldn't have sounded more reasonable. 'We had a deal; we both kept our ends of the bargain. Ain't got nothing to fight about.'

Ludza squinted down the sights.

'Come on now, Tillman.'

Some animal disturbed the brush at the far end of the yard; Ludza swung the rifle.

'We can build a fire,' he went on casually. 'Blacken up those goat nuts, grind 'em down and make some coffee. Reckon you must have a skillet inside, ain't you?'

Another movement in the brush, a crackle of dry leaves. Ludza steadied the Winchester. In the moonlight Tillman could see his finger on the trigger.

'Coffee sounds good, don't it?'

Ludza chuckled to himself, keeping up the charade.

'Hell if it don't. I tell you, I. . . .'

His voice fell away. There was a sharp movement in the brush, a snap of twigs, a crackle of dry leaves.

'Come on out where I can see you.'

A second later he fired. The shot ripped through the juniper leaves. Tillman heard him ratchet another shell into the barrel. A second shot tore into the underbrush. Then a third.

Ludza waited for a moment then, hearing nothing, levered himself up from where he crouched by the cabin wall. His Winchester aimed at the spot where the sounds had come from, he strode out across the yard and stopped just short of the trees.

'Damn you, Tillman,' he spat. 'Judge would have given me twice as much for handing you over alive.'

For good measure, he loosed off another round into the brush. Then three more in quick succcession.

Fifteen rounds in the magazine tube of a '73: everyone knew that. How many shots had Tillman heard him fire? Ten? Twelve maybe. Keeping his eyes on Ludza, Tillman reached down and felt for something to throw. He moved his hand slowly, careful not to make the slightest sound. But he needn't have worried. Ludza stood in front of the brush at the far end of the yard and stared at where his shots had gone. Something held him back from climbing in amongst the trees.

Tillman lobbed a stone so that it clattered against the cabin. Ludza wheeled. Two shots splintered into the wooden wall. Then there was silence broken only by the oiled, metallic sound of the Winchester lever working an empty magazine. A second later Tillman catapulted himself through the brush and out from behind the line of junipers.

'Hey, Ludza.'

Shocked by seeing someone he was convinced he'd just killed launch out into the ghostly moonlight, Ludza yelped like a puppy. Falling over himself to turn tail, he scrambled off towards the far side of the cabin. Rather than chase him into the shadows, Tillman hurried round the other side of the building to lay his hands on the .45. He could hear Ludza's stumbling footsteps, the sound of him trying to reload the magazine and his curses as the shells slipped through his fingers.

Round the back of the cabin, Tillman scanned the ground for the Colt. He had buried it with the $300, the sum Meckets paid when he bought him out of their partnership. Meckets offered more but Tillman wouldn't take it. After the Whipple tragedy, he didn't want anything from the ranch. He accepted the cash as insurance for June and changed his mind about the stock detective job so he would have the least possible contact with the other men. When he was about to set out on his first ride, he buried the money with the .45 and made sure June knew where it was.

'If anything happens to me, just remember ten paces from the back corner,' he told her.

They both knew there was always a chance that some trigger-happy rustler would ambush him. If the worst happened, June might need money or a handgun to defend herself, in addition to the scattergun they kept in the cabin.

Two shots from the Winchester sang through the night and tore into the juniper branches somewhere away to the left. Ludza had reloaded and was firing blind. Tillman scooted back across the yard, dived into the brush and hunkered down. A half-hour passed, maybe more. Ludza was trying to wait him out. Tillman checked the chamber of the .45. It was fully loaded and just as clean and oiled as the day he'd buried it. He found a goat nut in his pocket and started to chew.

A while later Ludza called out. He carried on a one-sided conversation about how they had a deal and how they should put foolishness aside; there was no need for them to shoot at each other. He started to move about somewhere behind the tree line at the far end of the yard, making a pretence of showing Tillman he had nothing to hide. Tillman stayed silent. He wondered what reward Ludza calculated on for the corpse of an escaped prisoner.

Tillman fought off the fatigue that weighed down on his shoulders. The inside of his eyelids felt coated with sand; his joints burned from sitting in the same position for so long. He struggled to keep his mind sharp, to listen out for the quietest footstep, to notice the smallest disturbance behind the trees. Whenever he heard a mouse patter in the dry leaves, his fingers tightened round the .45; if a night breeze moved the juniper branches, adrenaline jolted through him.

Since Ludza had not moved or called out for an hour by the time dull dawn light pushed across the eastern sky Tillman was convinced that he had fallen asleep. The dark outline of the cabin became visible; the tops of the junipers cut a ragged horizon against the new day. Tillman placed the .45 on the ground beside him, stretched his limbs and tried to flex the stiffness out of his joints. Just as he was wondering whether he could risk getting to his feet without giving himself away, a shot ripped through the leaves to his left.

Tillman threw himself flat; briers tore at his face. His right hand scrabbled for the .45 as a second shot splintered a juniper trunk two feet above his head. He lay still, his face buried in the dirt, his heart detonating behind his ribs. When the third shot didn't come he raised his head. He half expected to find himself staring down the barrel of Ludza's Winchester. But there was nothing, just the cabin, a hole in the ground, a pile of dirt and a shovel lying beside it.

A third shot ripped into the trees. Tillman flattened himself again. But the shot was further away this time. Then there was another, still further. Ludza was shooting at three-yard intervals along the line of junipers; he had no idea where Tillman was. This was an attempt to flush him out. The barrel of the Winchester appeared round the side of the cabin. Tillman sheltered the .45 with his left hand to deaden the sound as he thumbed back the hammer.

Just for a second, Ludza peered round the corner. It was enough time for Tillman to take a shot. Ludza yelped, dropped the Winchester and leaped back. Tillman levered himself to his feet. Expecting Ludza to make a dive for the rifle, he kept his .45 aimed and stepped out from the shelter of the brush.

The eastern sky was pale now; grey light flooded the yard. Mindful of the ease with which Ludza used his Bowie, Tillman trod noiselessly to the corner of the cabin, gun ready. To be doubly sure, he checked for movement behind the tree line in case Ludza doubled round behind him. At any second he expected Ludza to dive out and slash at him with his knife.

Keeping well back from the cabin wall, Tillman angled himself to get a view round the corner. No one. Empty air. And what looked like a bloodstain in the dirt. Instinct made Tillman wheel round, Ludza must be coming at him from behind. Again nothing, just the sway of the junipers in the morning breeze.

It was then that Tillman caught the sound of hoofbeats. He listened hard. Some way off but heading this way: three horses, he reckoned. Ludza had said the judge liked to know all about the men he condemned to hang; he must have found out where Tillman came from and figured this was where he would be headed.

Tillman looked around at the trees and wondered which of the branches could take his weight. The judge wouldn't waste time hauling him back to jail. He'd string him up from one of his own junipers.

4

Hoofbeats drummed on the track up from the ford; five minutes and the riders would be in the yard. Maybe it was a trick; maybe the judge had arranged to meet Ludza here. He could have sent him on ahead and told him to keep Tillman busy while he put together his hanging posse. Tillman imagined the noose around his neck; he felt the knot like a stone at the back of his head, felt the cattle rope scratch his skin the second before it cut off his air. He checked the chamber of the Colt. He had to get more ammunition. That meant getting himself inside the cabin.

Keeping low, Tillman exploded out of the brush and made a dive for the cabin wall. As he bit the dirt he expected shots from the Winchester. He snaked his way along the side of the building on his belly, .45 ready, eyes on the line of trees. When he reached the corner he peeped out into the yard. The horses still stood where they had been tethered the night before; there was water in the trough beside the well; nothing moved behind the junipers.

The posse's hoofs thundered closer. Tillman waited for them to crash through the brush, clothes covered in trail dust, guns in their hands, angry and unforgiving.

A story circulated in the jail that, once, when a prisoner managed to make it over the wall, the search party caught up with him, roped him like a steer and dragged him back by his feet behind the judge's horse. By the time they galloped through the main gate the man's head was severed. The judge dumped the bloody torso in the centre of the yard and ordered all the prisoners out of their cells on exercise to parade round it in the heat of the day.

Tillman made his break. Expecting a bullet to tear into his flesh, he hurled himself along the front wall of the cabin, flung open the wooden door and threw himself inside. The door banged behind him. To his amazement, he had made it.

As he picked himself up off the floor, Tillman had a strange sensation of having been propelled back into some former life. Nothing had been touched. June's quilt covered the bed; two chairs were pushed neatly under the table; a tub of cornmeal and a sack of salt were propped against the wall. A Dutch oven, an iron pan and a skillet, all shining clean, were arranged on the swept hearth. Above the bed, June had pinned her favourites from Tillman's sketches. A scattergun leaned against the wall by the door. The ashes of a fire lay in the grate. In the centre of the table a posy of jewel flowers had died, propped in a glass jar. The blackened petals lay where they had fallen; the stems had turned brittle, the water brackish.

Everything Tillman owned was here, just as he had left it the day the sheriff and his gang of leering deputies turned up to shout accusations in his face about him being a wife-killer and slam handcuffs on his wrists. He had been standing right here when they careered into the yard. The coffee pot he had just filled when the door burst open was still sitting on the hearth; the bedroll he had dropped was on the floor beside the bed; lying on the table was the sketch book filled with drawings he made while he watched the herd the day before.

On his hands and knees, Tillman heaved a wooden chest out from under the bed. Under June's neatly folded Sunday clothes and the spare shirt and pants she kept ready for him, were boxes of slugs for the .45 and shells for the scattergun. He ducked below the window line, snatched the scattergun, broke open the breech and fed a cartridge into each barrel. Then he rechecked the chamber of his .45.

Tillman risked a peek from one corner of the window. Nothing. The horses were still tethered. The yard was still empty. But it was quiet. No hoofbeats. The posse should be there now; he should be able to hear them breaking through the trees. Another second and they should be out there all lined up against him, pumping lead into the cabin walls, shooting out the door and windows. He moved to the other side of the window to get a different angle on the yard. No one. The juniper branches moved slightly in a morning breeeze; the horses stood patiently by the well.

Then someone called his name.

'Tillman, you in there?'

At first he couldn't place the voice. It wasn't Ludza: the voice was ground glass. It couldn't be the judge: he wouldn't waste time calling out; he would send his men straight in. Sheriff Hoyt, the man who had arrested him? Tillman struggled to remember what his voice sounded like; all he could remember was his laugh, a piglet squeal: it couldn't be him. This voice was dark and tobacco-stained, used to barking orders and commanding obedience, deep, abrupt and angry.

'Tillman.' The voice slammed like a door. 'I ain't asking again.'

Tillman propped the loaded scattergun against the wall and thumbed back the hammer of the .45. He knew who it was. He peered from the edge of the window again and ducked back quickly. Still no one in the yard.

'Word is you busted out of jail the night before you was due to hang. Didn't expect you to be crazy enough to come back here but I reckoned I'd best check your old place.'

There was still no movement in the yard. The men were keeping back behind the trees but Tillman couldn't say exactly where. No chance he could get to his horse before their bullets cut him down. Even if he was able to scramble up into the saddle, he didn't have a cat's chance of making it beyond the junipers.

'Doing the judge's dirty work now, Meckets?' Tillman's voice was calm. 'You know I'll shoot any of the men you send in here. You told 'em that?'

Meckets, ranch boss, owner of the largest herd of long-horn-cross in the state, Tillman's employer, Tillman's father-in-law, Tillman's former friend. The man who had handed him over to the law; the man Tillman had to convince he was innocent.

'Same old Tillman.' Meckets sneered; his voice carried across the yard. 'Dug yourself into a hole, too stubborn to dig yourself out.'

Tillman let the insult ride.

'Come on out, Tillman,' Meckets boomed. 'You ain't got a choice. I can sit here all day.'

Just for a second Tillman saw movement behind the trees. Hardly visible in the brush, someone on foot crossed in front of the cabin. Tillman ducked to the other side of the window, .45 ready. There was disturbance behind the junipers, the flicker of a shadow between the trees. Meckets had ordered his men to spread out.

'Why don't you and me talk?' Tillman called. 'We can sort this out, just the two of us.'

Meckets' laugh was like an echo in a cave.

'This ain't the old days, Tillman; this ain't you and me. You're a convicted killer. You shot my daughter and I intend to see you swing for it.'

Tillman's stomach turned to water. Standing in the cabin, everything reminded him of June: the quilt he'd watched her sew, the pans she'd cleaned until they shone, the posy she'd placed in the centre of the table to welcome him home, the shirts she'd washed and folded for him. With his memories weighing down on him, he thought his legs were going to buckle. He leaned his weight against the wall and stared round the edge of the window. Movement shook the trees, running footsteps crashed through the brush. Meckets' men had given up trying to hide.

'Come on out,' Meckets shouted. 'You've been convicted by a court of law. Come on out and face justice.'

Meckets wanted him alive. Tillman realized that now. At first he thought Meckets was going to have his men storm the cabin and gun him down. But if he'd wanted to do that, the shooting would have started. He wanted to hand him over to the judge and hear his neck snap.

One of the men was at the back of the cabin, Tillman heard him scratching at the timber wall. What was he doing: trying to break through? Then he heard him curse and the sound of his boots slip as he hoisted himself up on to the roof. His footsteps echoed; each one shook the joists. He trod cautiously; dessicated by months of heat, there was a chance the cottonwood planks would give way.

Meckets called out again.

'Hell with this, Tillman.' Anger burned his voice. 'I ain't gonna let you play me.'

The man on the roof started to lever at one of the cottonwood boards. The nails screeched in protest.

'Throw out your gun and walk out of that door with your hands up,' Meckets yelled. Ludicrous. No chance Tillman would ever give in to an ultimatum like that; Meckets was trying to distract him.

On the roof the man worked his way along; Tillman heard him grunt with the effort of it. Through the window, it was lighter now; Tillman made out the silhouettes of Meckets's men in the spaces between the trees. He counted four.

'You make me come in there, you're a dead man,' Meckets yelled.

Tillman heard exasperation tear at Meckets's voice. Shocked that someone had the nerve to stand up to him, his fury was barely controlled.

Something cracked like a pistol shot above Tillman's head. Tillman threw himself against the wall to get out of the line of fire. But it wasn't a shot. A man's leg thrust through the cabin roof, a scuffed boot and torn work pants stuck down into the room as the boards gave way. Gun in hand, Tillman made a dive for the leg and swung on it. Above him, a man roared with pain and shock as the cottonwood splintered. He crashed through and landed in a heap of dust and broken timber on the cabin floor. Tillman recognized Brewster, one of Meckets's cattle hands, a fleshy guy with a reputation for raising hell. Tillman lunged forward, caught him in a headlock, hauled him to his feet and kept his .45 pressed against his temple before he had a chance to realize what was happening. Brewster thrashed wildly to get away but the headlock choked him; his hands scrabbled to try to lever Tillman's arm away from his windpipe.

'Meckets,' Tillman yelled. 'I'm coming out. Hold your fire, hear me?'

'Heard you.' Meckets' voice came from somewhere behind the trees.

Still with his arm across Brewster's throat, Tillman frog-marched him across the cabin floor, kicked the door open and booted him out into the yard. At the same time, he flung himself back inside. As the door swung shut, a storm of bullets from Meckets's men cut Brewster down.

Tillman grabbed the shotgun, dragged the table across to under where the roof was caved in, clambered up on it, found a joist that would take his weight and hauled himself up. Out on the roof, a second later, he saw Meckets, Harlan, and a couple more ranch hands emerge from the trees, .45s in their hands, and dash across the yard to where Brewster's body lay splayed in the blood-stained dirt.

Meckets's curses damned his men to hell as Tillman slid down the pitch of the roof and landed on his feet at the back of the cabin. He heard the door bang open, more yelling and boot heels stamping on the wooden floor as he slipped round the side. He knew that in a second one of them would be climbing out through the hole in the roof. With an eye on the cabin door he hurried across the yard to where his horse was tethered, slipped the reins and climbed up into the saddle.

The barrage of shouting and blame continued inside the cabin. Tillman recognized Harlan's voice as he tried to stand up to his uncle. Then Meckets dashed outside. As he caught sight of Tillman, he tripped on Brewster's twisted corpse. He fired as Tillman's appaloosa leapt forward. The shot angled wide. Tillman careered into the trees followed by more wild shooting. He heard Meckets's voice roar above the others.

'You killed my daughter, Tillman. I'm gonna see you hang.'

The sun was almost up now. Gold light burst from behind the horizon; sketches of blood-red cirrus arced high in the pale sky. Tillman wheeled the pony and hurried along behind the junipers parallel with the cabin. He knew where the men would have tethered their horses. He heard them heading there now, blundering through the trees. He reached the spot at the edge of the junipers where the reins of a group of cow ponies and Meckets's bay were looped around the lower branches. He reached down from the saddle, freed each one and herded them towards the slope and down to the valley.

After a mile Tillman cut away from the ponies. He let them gallop away, exuberant with their new found freedom in the cool morning air. When he was sure they weren't going to turn back towards their owners, he cut a wide arc and, after another mile, headed back in the direction of the cabin.

In the distance, Tillman counted three figures heading down the hillside in pursuit of their mounts. That left Meckets on his own. Then something else struck him: Ludza's horse was gone when Tillman broke out of the cabin. Had he high-tailed it back to his quarters at the jail with the bundle of cash in his pocket? More likely, he had gone to track down the judge and his posse, full of some cock-and-bull story about having cornered Tillman only to have him slip away in the night.

Tillman suddenly became aware of how hungry he was. He felt in his pocket. He was down to his last goat nut. When he bit into it, the flesh was woody and sour. He remembered the barrel of cornmeal back at the cabin and how June would make a batch of Johnny cakes every time he set out for the herd. It was how she said goodbye. She would hand him a cup of coffee and he would watch as she arranged the cornmeal patties on a barrel lid and then prop it in front of the fire. He remembered how attentive she was to see that the cakes were baked just right, how she would adjust the angle of the lid and move it closer to the heat or further away.

The cabin used to become filled with the smell of roast coffee and baking cornmeal. June would ask him how many days he was going to be away this time, tell him to keep himself safe and hurry home. She would go through all the things she had bundled up for him, a change of clothes, a bedroll, his canteens. Last of all she would hand him his sketch book and a fistful of pencils and tell him to bring her back some drawings. Then she would laugh and say she guessed no one in the territory had more sketches of longhorns than she had. Tillman would laugh with her and playfully ask if that didn't make her feel lucky. She would smile her shy smile, look him in the eye and say yes, it did.

Tillman had never been happier. June was the love of his life. How could anyone believe that he ever wanted to harm a hair on her head? And here he was, sentenced to hang for shooting her, point blank. Something cracked inside him when he remembered. His strength drained; it was as much as he could do to stop himself falling.

Images of him and June filled his head. He remembered

how they liked nothing better than to saddle up and make an evening ride down into the valley while the air was still warm and the blazing sun painted the sky. He remembered her joyous laughter, how she loved the excitement of the gallop, how she rode alongside him and shouted a conversation as their horses carried them along the bank of the stream.

At other times June would catch him unawares and gallop way ahead, so he had to ride hard to keep up with her. She looked beautiful with her skin honeyed by the sun and her long hair tucked up under his old hat, which she had taken to wearing; it was thrilling to have her alongside him.

Right now Tillman forced these thoughts out of his head and headed back towards the cabin. By the time he got close to the line of junipers he had lost sight of Harlan and the other two. He dismounted quietly, tethered his pony to a low branch and picked his way through the brush. He trod slowly, pausing after each footstep to let the sound settle. Peering through the trees, he saw that the cabin door was closed and the yard was empty. He crouched low and listened. Surely Meckets would assume he had made a break for it and was miles away by now; he wouldn't think he would double back, would he? Meckets must be inside.

There was no sound out here, not the snap of a twig, no movement in the dry leaves. Above him, the branches shifted slightly in a morning breeze, that was all.

The cabin door banged open. Tillman froze. Meckets strolled out and took a seat on the edge of the porch. With his gun in its holster, he settled down to leaf through Tillman's sketch book, which he had picked up from the table inside. Every now and then he would hold up a drawing and squint at it through half-shut eyes. Then he would put the book back on his lap and continue to flick over the pages. When he'd finished he went back and found one or two particular sketches, he took a moment to stare at them again. As he put the book down beside him, Tillman broke through the brush.

Meckets's hand went for his gun but, faced with Tillman's .45 levelled at his chest, he let his hand drop to his side. Shock bleached his face and his stare was merciless.

'You dare to come back here?' Meckets growled.

'Come back to prove I'm an innocent man,' Tillman said simply.

'You're scum, Tillman.' The edges of Meckets's mouth sloped down; his face was cast in steel. 'I'm gonna see you hang.'

5

Tillman had first run into Meckets the week he arrived in Arizona territory. One evening he walked into a saloon in Tuscon where a big-built guy stood at the bar with his thumbs in his vest pockets and a steel watch-chain across his belly. Tillman heard him call for a round for the room and demand to know if anyone knew of vacant land suitable for a cattle ranch. He said that as soon as he staked a claim he would be back to hire hands, but the guys in the saloon were suspicious. They were wise to tricksters who promised to pay at the end of the season, after the cattle had been sold on. Itinerant cattle herders, full of sorry tales of having lost everything in the war, had a habit of disappearing with the payroll before they settled with the hired men. This Texan with his big ideas was too good to be true.

New in town, Tillman didn't know a soul in the place, and as Meckets was cold-shouldered by the other drinkers the two of them fell to talking. As they listened to each other's stories, each recognized something in the other that drew them together. They both wanted to put down roots. Meckets needed a partner he could rely on; Tillman had no better place to be. Like everyone else, the war had destroyed their lives. Back in Texas, Meckets had returned from the army to find his wife dead from consumption and his teenage daughter being cared for by a neighbour. Tillman had no family; he needed a new start.

When war broke out, Tillman had been drifting south, taking odd jobs and sketching the portraits of anyone who would pay him. Like Meckets, he signed up at the recruiting office of the town he was in at the time. For both of them, life had been a matter of survival. They each had the idea that they needed to join the army to defend themselves and what little they owned; the wider politics of which side was right or wrong got lost. The result was that they endured five years of bloody hell, and when it was over tried to pick up where they left off: Tillman trailed from farm to farm with no more possessions than his precious sketch books and the clothes he wore on his back; Meckets headed home to track down his family and gather up what was left of his herd.

On his wanderings Tillman had passed through a valley in the foothills of the granite mountains to the south, where there was fresh water and ready pasture. He suggested it was the kind of place Meckets was looking for. To get there you had to cross a corner of the Sonora close to where the Prescott legislature had ordered a jailhouse to be built and placed under the jurisdiction of a hanging judge. It was intended to deter the gunslingers and cattle-thieves whose rampages threatened to reduce the area to anarchy. The following day, the two men rode out there.

The first year after Meckets staked his claim was hard. He threw himself into his work; he knew this was his chance to make it rich and he determined to chase every opportunity that opened up. He hired cow hands, expanded the herd and led a long drive north to the railhead. With his natural facility for cutting a deal he made a big profit. Added to that, he, Harlan and Tillman built a cabin out of timber they felled themselves on the ridge overlooking the valley. For months they all lived together, with June keeping everyone fed and helping out at round-up time.

With cash flow rising steeply during the second year, Meckets hired extra labour and built a ranch house on the opposite head of the valley. A few months later Tillman and June got hitched. At the same time Tillman decided to cut loose from the partnership with Meckets. It had been on his mind for months. Although the money was good, the role of managing a ranch didn't suit him. He hated the hiring and firing and was ill at ease pressing deals with flint-eyed cattle traders; trying to be a businessman went against the grain. The final straw was the terrible business of Frank Whipple's death. After that Tillman wanted the open range and a peaceful way of life that would bring happiness to June and himself. Nothing more, nothing less.

From where Meckets stood Tillman lacked ambition. Arizona territory was wide open, even a fool could see that. Granted, you had to be thick-skinned to get the most out of Mexican labour and when you went about annexing former Apache land; but if you were hard headed enough your fortune was guaranteed. But it was obvious that Tillman and June were head over heels. He'd seen them heading off for evening walks together along the stream and noticed how cheerful June became whenever Tillman was due home after a day out with the herd. Plainly, building a cattle business was the last thing on Tillman's mind. Added to this, Meckets was well aware that June had inherited his stubborn streak; if he objected to the match, most likely she and Tillman would disappear off to California and he would never see her again.

With an eye to the main chance as usual, Meckets figured out a way of keeping June and Tillman happy and turning the situation to his advantage. He offered to buy Tillman out of the partnership and take him on as a stock detective. Now the new ranch house was built, he also offered to let them have the old cabin to live in as a wedding present. The cabin would be a home for June; Tillman would have his freedom from the business; Meckets would have a stock detective he could trust and his daughter would still be close. In the back of his mind, he believed that, sooner or later, Tillman would get fed up with spending his days out on the range and want to buy his way back into partnership. Meckets was confident that when that day came, he would be able to broker a deal that would keep Tillman and June happy and show a profit for himself.

'Throw your gun down,' Tillman snapped.

Meckets stared at him, cold-eyed with fury. Tillman knew that look.

'Right now.'

'Remember when you first came to me?' Meckets said.

'Real slow,' Tillman said. 'On the ground in front of you.'

Meckets didn't take his eyes off him.

'Asked me for a job and I took you on. Biggest mistake of my life.'

He moved his hand to his holster, palmed the .45 and let it fall down into the dirt.

Tillman kicked the gun aside. For a second he thought Meckets might make a grab for him. The cattleman might be ten years his senior, but he was hard-muscled and

56

tough. His stare was murderous.

'Never thought it would come to this. Should have left you in that saloon along with all those other no-hopers.'

'I'm going to say this once.' Tillman holstered his gun. His face was grave and his words were clear and precise. 'I didn't kill June. You know me. You know I could never do a thing like that.'

Was there a waver in his voice? Tillman kept his composure even though merely having to say June's name made the strength go out of him.

'You're convicted by a court of law,' Meckets said. 'Why waste your breath lying?'

'That night—' Tillman started to explain.

'I said, why waste your breath?' Meckets looked daggers. 'Harlan and the boys will be back here soon. You know how trigger-happy Harlan is. Don't make any difference if you shoot me or you don't, he'll still come after you.'

Harlan had been a sixteen-year-old kid when Tillman first met him. Meckets brought him on the drive from Texas partly because he needed another hand and partly to make a man of his nephew. From what Tillman could see, Harlan had always been a brat. An only child, he turned out spoiled and lazy. His pa, Meckets's brother, begged Meckets to let him ride along.

With memories of his late wife still burning inside him, Meckets was pleased to take Harlan on; he was going to be the son they'd never had.

For a while he believed Harlan would become heir to the fortune he was going to make. He doted on him. He persuaded himself that his nephew's short temper was an intelligent refusal to suffer fools; he made out that the

57

dismissive way he spoke to the hired hands showed he was a born leader; he thought his spitefulness was merely a young buck asserting himself. Meckets was only right about one thing: Harlan was trigger-happy.

As far as Tillman was concerned, he made it his business to give Harlan a wide berth. He recognized Meckets's fondness for his kin and would have respected it, even if the young man had been the least deserving on earth. He kept out of Harlan's way. When Meckets made him partner he made sure that Harlan knew all decisions were taken jointly; when they were out with the herd, he made a point of giving Harlan easier jobs; when they were in Tuscon and Harlan had money in his pocket, Tillman never went near the saloon.

The one issue that made Tillman confront Harlan was the way he ill-treated the Mexican hands. Tillman wouldn't stand for it. Without telling Meckets, he cornered Harlan one night in the hay barn and spelled it out for him. The sniping, the put-downs and the constant mockery all had to stop. The hands might let it ride because Harlan was the boss's nephew, but he wouldn't.

Harlan's reaction was superior and sneering. He made a few wild accusations about Tillman only marrying June so that Meckets kept him on as stock detective, but both of them knew this was blatantly untrue. As far as Tillman was concerned, it was water off a duck's back.

Tillman knew about Harlan's teenage crush on June. He figured that Harlan was jealous of him and this made him go easier on him than he would otherwise have done. But it didn't make Harlan any less resentful. Spoilt as a kid, given more responsibility than he could handle by Meckets, let down lightly by June and now allowed to slip off the hook once more, Harlan's resentment of Tillman grew into loathing. And he didn't try to hide it.

Meckets glared at Tillman as though he wanted to rip out his throat with his bare hands. Tillman breathed deep and tried again.

'That night,' he said, 'June wasn't home.'

'Hell with you,' Meckets snarled. 'Don't you try to weasel out of nothing. You think I don't know what happened?'

'When I got back from the high land above the ridge—' Tillman continued.

'I know that,' Meckets thundered. 'She'd been over at the ranch all day. It was hours before she would tell me what the matter was. She'd been crying because you had filled her head with some fool notion. Cooked up a pile of lies about Harlan, her own cousin, for mercy's sake. Everyone knows you never liked him, right from when you two first met.'

'I told her the truth,' Tillman said. 'Told her I suspected Harlan and some of the men had been cutting the herd. Said I planned to find out exactly who before I reported it to you and the sheriff.'

'That's a lie.' Meckets' words fell like a hammer. 'You expect me to believe my own nephew would steal from me?'

'I figured out what they were doing,' Tillman went on. 'Cut the herd at the south end of the valley, waited for a dark night, drove 'em through Stealer's at sundown and down to the border. Must've arranged for someone to wait down there.'

'Take care what you say.' Meckets's voice was almost a whisper. 'You murdered my daughter and now you're accusing my nephew.'

'I knew it was Harlan by his horse,' Tillman persisted. 'I could make it out. That chestnut you bought for him must stand at sixteen hands. The guys with him rode cow ponies; I couldn't tell one from another.'

'Enough,' Meckets yelled. His eyes slid to where his .45 lay in the dirt over to his right. 'You spouted this nonsense at your trial. The judge didn't believe you, so why should I?'

For a second, Tillman thought Meckets was about to launch himself at him. He took a pace back.

'You hurt June real bad, so she did what all girls do when their husband picks on them.' Meckets stared at him. 'She ran home. Wouldn't even tell me what it was at first, and I'm her pa. I just had to stand there and watch her sob her heart out.'

'I warned June what was going to happen,' Tillman said. 'Told her I had to go out and catch Harlan along with the others.'

'You met her when she was riding home and you shot her.' Meckets voice trembled.

'I'm telling you the judge was wrong,' Tillman insisted.

'I thought I knew you.' Meckets stared at him. 'I trusted you. Let you marry my daughter. You turned on me like a rattlesnake, on all of us. Me, Harlan, and you put a bullet in June.'

The sound of hoofbeats made both men look up.

'Looks like your plan didn't work.' A sneer twisted Meckets's mouth. 'Sounds like Harlan chased down the horses.'

Tillman's stomach lurched. How could he ever have believed he would convince Meckets? This had been a waste of time; he should have run; he should have climbed up on his horse and put as much ground between him and this place as he could. If this was Harlan and his men they would shoot him straight off; if it was the judge, he would put a rope round his neck, no question.

Then another thought entered Tillman's head. If they were coming for him, let them come. He had never run from anything in his life and he wasn't about to start now.

He walked over and picked up Meckets's gun.

'Gonna shoot me with my own weapon?' Meckets flinched. 'Is that what this has come to?'

'If there's going to be gunplay, you best get out of here,' Tillman gestured Meckets to get to his feet. 'I'm keeping your .45.'

'Just because you don't put a slug in me don't mean I won't chase you down,' Meckets said.

'Get out of here.' Tillman gestured to the direction of the hoofbeats.

Meckets heaved himself to his feet. With a last, uncertain look over his shoulder he hurried away into the trees. The sky was pale now; light had spread from the east and already the sun had begun to warm the air. A pair of red-tails slid through the thermals, assessing the landscape, calculating where they might find their first victim of the day.

The sound of the hoofbeats stopped. Maybe someone riding point had spotted Meckets; maybe whoever it was had decided to circle the ranch; maybe they were coming on foot. As Tillman turned to head into the cabin he stooped down to pick up the sketch book from where Meckets had let it fall in the dirt.

This was the sketch book Tillman had taken with him on the day of the shooting. He carried one like it in his saddle-bag together with a bundle of pencils every time he rode out. Sometimes the drawings were of individual beeves, sometimes they were of horses, sometimes they showed the wide sweep of the landscape. They could be detailed studies, scraps of sketches or doodles of things that caught his eye. He had always drawn things. The feeling of calm that sketching gave him was unlike anything else he ever felt; it made him feel part of things, focused his vision and enabled him to see details that otherwise would have passed him by.

Some evenings, Tillman flicked through the pages he had worked on; often he never did. Once he met a businessman who wanted to know why he never worked up his sketches into paintings, started going on about something he called 'untutored technique' and talked about exhibitions in Boston galleries. The idea of putting his pictures of Meckets's longhorns in gold frames for a bunch of rich folks to hang over their mantelpieces made Tillman smile. His drawings were instinctive, quick, and doing them was as natural to him as breathing; they were his way of looking; his way of understanding what was really there.

The book fell open at the last page. It was a drawing of the herd from the top of the ridge above the cabin. Underneath were the words *Getting Near Sundown, Stealer's Creek* and the date. One glance at the sketch and anger reared up in him like bile. He slung the book across the room. The pages fluttered like wings; it landed face down, splayed open. While he was up on the ridge making this drawing, someone shot his wife.

Meckets had been quick to send one of the hands to fetch the sheriff and have him arrested. At the trial he testified that there had been an argument, June was distraught and ran home. The sheriff's evidence was that Tillman raged with anger when he came to arrest him. Harlan testified that he heard shots from the direction of the ford. Whipple said that when he saw Tillman carry June's body into the ranch house he looked as if he had come to confess. In addition, everyone knew what an accurate shot Tillman was and the two shots through June's heart were closely grouped.

Tillman had barely been able to grasp that people he knew would set out to see him hang, but they had. No one believed him. Blinded by grief for June, Meckets had turned on him; petty jealousy had spurred Harlan on; Whipple had hated him. Tillman looked round the cabin as if this was the last time he might see it. He looked up at the hole Brewster tore in the roof. He hadn't got the stomach for running any more.

Instead, Tillman stripped off the prison guard's uniform he had worn since the break-out and fished his own clothes out of the chest under the bed. He kicked off the borrowed boots and pulled on his own. The clean cotton felt good against his skin. He shoved the two Colts, his and Mecketss's, into his belt and sat down by the window to wait. This was what June would have wanted him to do: make a stand, face down his enemies, talk to them for as long as it took. If that failed, she would have wanted him to take his chances with a gun.

Opposite the window a pair of redstarts hopped between the branches of the junipers, gleaning insects from the leaves. Their scarlet feathers flashed like splashes of blood. At the sound of footsteps smashing through the brush, they flew to a higher branch. Tillman pulled his .45

from his belt.

There was a shout.

'Got the place surrounded, Tillman. No way to escape.'
Ludza.

'Judge is right behind me. Wants to string you up.'

Tillman scanned the trees.

'Gonna be here in a couple of minutes. Met up with
that ranch boss too, the guy you used to work for. He's on
his way. You should have shot him while you had the
chance. He hates you, Tillman.' Ludza laughed briefly.
'Can't blame him, seeing as you killed his daughter. No
one could expect mercy for that.'

Then Tillman realized something.

'You on your own, Ludza?' he called.

'Said I'd ride on ahead. Told the judge, if anyone had a
chance of getting you to come out, it was me. You gonna
come out, Tillman, or are you gonna let them gun you
down like vermin?'

The redstarts hopped from branch to branch, scarlet
feathers against the juniper leaves.

'You want that extra three hundred before the
Governor comes?' Tillman called. 'Ain't no good to me
now.'

There was movement behind the trees. Ludza was listening.

'I got all your money. You had it buried. I ain't gonna
let you put a bullet in me, Tillman.'

'It's right here in the chest under the bed. You want it,
you'll have to come in and get it. I ain't moving from this
window.'

The underbrush shifted suddenly as though a dog had
been disturbed.

'You don't come in and collect it, judge's boys are

gonna help themselves first chance they get.'

'How do I know you ain't gonna shoot me?' Ludza said.

'Another three hundred,' Tillman called out. 'If you want it, you'll have to come for it right now.'

6

Tillman kept his eyes on the tree line. For a while the junipers were still and nothing moved in the brush. As the redstarts became confident again they hopped from branch to branch; vermilion feathers flagged a warning.

'Why are you doing this?' Ludza sounded uneasy, but greed had the better of him. He didn't care about the answer, he just wanted to know that Tillman wasn't going to shoot him if he stepped out from his cover into the yard.

'It's what you asked for.' Tillman's reply was matter of fact, as though it was obvious.

Another silence followed, longer this time, while Ludza worked on a plan. Eventually he called out again.

'Wouldn't shoot an unarmed man, would you?' There was deliberate hesitation in his voice, a false innocence.

'Never have yet.' Tillman knew what was coming.

'Throwing out my rifle,' Ludza called.

The Winchester landed with a thud out in the yard.

'Got your word you won't shoot me, ain't I?'

'You got it.'

Opposite the cabin door Ludza pushed the brush aside and stepped out. In a flash of feathers the redstarts flew higher up the trees. Ludza's guard's uniform was dirt-stained; his face was thin. He raised his hand in a wave towards the cabin while he struggled to hold a smile on his mouth. As he took his first nervous step, his eyes darted between the window and the cabin door.

'Ain't got all day,' Tillman called.

Ludza took a few cautious steps, as though he was trying not to put his weight on the ground. Halfway across the yard he lost his nerve.

'Throw it out. I ain't coming no further.'

'Another three hundred,' Tillman said. 'In the chest under the bed.'

'Helped you out, didn't I?' Ludza's smile angled across his mouth. 'Let you escape the day before you was due to hang. You owe me for that. You ain't gonna do nothing stupid, are you?'

He started towards the cabin door again. Tillman waited until he stepped inside.

'Where is it?' Ludza sounded as though he had just won a poker hand and wanted everyone to know.

'Had to lie to you about the three hundred,' Tillman said. 'Just like you lied to me about not telling the judge. Reckon you intended to take my money then hand me over and claim a reward. Or maybe you intended to shoot me first.'

The smile slid from Ludza's face. His mouth opened to say something just as Tillman's fist exploded against his jaw. Ludza lurched backwards, staggered as his legs jellied, and collapsed against the bin of cornmeal. He groaned, his eyelids fluttered and his mouth sagged open.

Without a second glance at the crumpled Ludza Tillman grabbed the scattergun and turned for the door. Crossing the yard, he scooped up the Winchester and lobbed it casually into the brush. He unhitched Ludza's pony and hurried her into the trees. The one thought in his head was that if he could get to the ranch he might be able to find someone who knew what had happened on the night of the shooting. Maybe one of the hands had seen something; maybe he could try to talk to Meckets again, or even Harlan. Faint hope, he knew that. But what else could he try? He took a last look back. The cabin door was open; he could see Ludza slumped on the floor.

The ranch house was an hour's ride. Tillman ignored the twist of hunger in his guts and headed for his appaloosa tethered on the other side of the trees. As he slipped the scattergun into the saddle holster, a voice called out.

'Hey, Ludza, is he still in there?' It was Meckets's voice. Tillman drew his .45. 'Did you see him?'

Tillman froze.

'Boys ain't back with the horses,' Meckets went on. 'I'm sick of waiting, I can tell you.'

His voice came from somewhere to the left, the place where Harlan and the others had tethered their horses.

'Hey,' Meckets called out. 'Can you hear me?'

Tillman pushed his way through the underwood until there was only a curtain of creosote bush between him and Meckets. Meckets sat on the ground with his back to Tillman, hand shading his eyes, staring out across the valley.

As Tillman broke through the brush he pulled back the hammer of his .45. Meckets swung round and stumbled to his feet. His eyes were wide with shock; his hands scrabbled helplessly with the brush as he tried to back away.

'You come to kill me?'

His voice shook. Tillman had never seen him afraid before.

'Sit down.' Tillman gestured with the .45. 'And listen.'

Meckets slid down the trunk of one of the junipers and stared up at him. As he realized that Tillman wasn't going to shoot him colour returned to his face.

'Listen?' he sneered. 'You got something to say you better hurry up. Judge's hanging posse will be here real soon; if it ain't the judge, it'll be Harlan and the boys. Everyone wants you dead, Tillman, and all you want to do is talk. Then there's that fool prison guard who reckons he's about to cash in on some reward. I didn't hear no shots so he must be alive somewhere. You seen the size of that Bowie he carries? He'll gut you as quick as drawing breath.'

'Shut up.'

Tillman kept his .45 aimed straight at Meckets's chest. Meckets stared at him.

'I rode out on to the ridge so I could have a view over Stealer's,' Tillman began. 'The herd was in the low land by the river. I could see everything from up there. . . .'

'Not this again,' Meckets snarled. 'You couldn't convince the judge; what makes you think you've got a cat in hell's chance of convincing me?'

'You testified against me,' Tillman said. 'You've known me for years. Why would you do that?'

'What are you implying?' The colour drained from Mecket's face. 'You making out I killed my own daughter? Is that your story now?'

Tillman hesitated. There were words in his head but he couldn't make them into sense. He didn't have a story. All he had was questions.

'I was watching from the high ground this side of the

69

river. In the south, rustlers were working on a split. Couldn't see who they were, too far away. All I could make out was the dust cloud kicked up by cattle moving down to Stealer's.'

'Harlan and the boys were out with the herd,' Meckets said wearily. 'They never saw nothing.'

'Someone rode out from the ranch house and went to join 'em,' Tillman went on.

'Join Harlan?' Meckets tried to follow what he was saying.

'That's right,' Tillman said. 'Rode south.'

'This is bull.' Meckets said. 'The only people in the ranch house was me and June. Joe Whipple was working in the forge out back; the rest of the boys were with the herd. When June left she headed home. She told me. You ran into her on the way and that's when you shot her.'

The accusation twisted a blade in Tillman's guts. It weakened him like a wound through which his strength bled out. He imagined June's face, her sweet smile. He remembered how she left the cabin door open around the time he was due home so she could look out for him; he remembered how she came running out when she heard hoofbeats in the yard.

When he got home that terrible evening the cabin was closed up and the yard was empty. Her horse was still in the barn, so, at first, Tillman thought she must be somewhere near by and just hadn't heard him. He remembered calling out to her and hearing his words echo; he remembered thinking how strange it was that she didn't answer. Then he realized that although her horse was there, the old cow pony they kept was missing and June's saddle wasn't in its usual place on the side of the stall.

In the cabin his old plainsman hat, the one she borrowed so she could tuck her long hair up underneath it, was missing from the peg by the door. She used to help herself to it when she intended to ride hard and knew she would kick up a storm of dust. Ashes were cold in the fire grate; there was no food ready.

Tillman wasn't worried at first. June was a strong rider; what could have happened? Mindful of the news he had broken to her that morning, he remembered how at first she had reacted with flat disbelief. Then tears had welled in her eyes as he explained his suspicions and told her what he intended to do. He told her he reckoned Harlan was splitting her father's herd, driving the cattle a few head at a time through Stealer's Creek and south to the border. He had told her he was going to keep watch from the high ridge. It must have preyed on her mind all day.

'You filled her head with poison,' Meckets said. 'Made her believe her own cousin was stealing from the family herd. June was a sweet-natured girl, never thought badly of anyone. Then you worked on her. She was upset; took hours before she told me what the matter was. In the end she couldn't hold it in no longer; told me your wild accusations about Harlan. When you met her at the ford that night she stood up to you, she took her family's side and you killed her for it. Sooner the judge gets here and puts a rope around your neck the better.'

Meckets anger was palpable; he was set on revenge. 'You're a fool, Tillman. You got everything upside down. Why should Harlan steal from me? One day this whole shooting match will be his.'

Tillman searched the sky to the north for a telltale dust cloud which would mean the judge's posse was closing. But there was nothing, just the bright morning sky and thin, high cirrus. To the south the land opened out

71

between the two bluffs, the stream emerged from the rock like a miracle, swung south down the centre of the valley and encouraged meadow grass to carpet the land, where only half a mile to the north the desert floor was sand and dry dirt.

'I found her body in the ford,' Tillman persisted. His words were so quiet, it sounded like a confession. He spoke to himself rather than Meckets, as if he was explaining what he had seen to make sure he understood. 'On the road between the cabin and the ranch house.'

'What the hell are you telling me this for?' Meckets shuddered.

'She was face down,' Tillman went on. 'There was a cloud of her blood in the water. The pony was standing over her, waiting for her to get up. At first, I thought he'd thrown her. I thought she was going to get to her feet and laugh. The horse wasn't used to her; her own horse had lost a shoe, that's why she took this one from the barn.'

'I don't want to listen to this,' Meckets snapped. 'I heard it all at the trial, you pleading that when you got there she was already dead. Judge didn't believe you; no one did.'

'Why should I do a thing like that? What possible reason could there be?' Tillman's voice was little more than a whisper; the gun wavered in his hand.

'Judge said you were riled because you'd told her not to ride over to the ranch, not to speak to me or Harlan or anyone until you came back with proof. When you met her on the road and she told you where she'd been, you got angry. June fought back; she wasn't going to settle for you bad-mouthing her kin, even if you were her husband. That was when you pulled your gun on her.'

'You believe that?' Tillman's face was jagged with grief.

'I believe you're scum, Tillman. I wish I'd never set eyes on you. I should have stopped you courting June but she was so darn headstrong, she would argue black was white, if she had a mind to . . .'

Meckets broke off; no amount of rancour directed at Tillman made him feel better.

Tillman kept his .45 trained on Meckets and sat down with his back against the trunk of a juniper. He didn't know how to convince him.

'How did you bust out of jail anyway?' Meckets said.

'Never mind that.' Tillman stared at him. 'If I was guilty I would have high-tailed it, wouldn't I? Instead of that I'm sitting here trying to convince you of the truth.'

Meckets slid a tin of Bull Durham from his shirt pocket, put a plug between his teeth and started to chew.

'Convince away,' he said casually, as though nothing Tillman could say mattered. 'Better make it quick. Posse will be here soon.'

He stared deliberately out into the desert, as though he couldn't bring himself to rest his eyes on the other man.

In Tillman's head the images from that night were as clear as if they had happened five minutes ago. It was dusk. The cabin was closed up. No lights; the grate was cold. When he called June's name, there was no answer. The barn door was shut; June's horse had eaten all her feed. It looked as though the place had been empty all day.

Whenever Tillman returned home, June always had chow ready. On baking days the rich smell of fresh sourdough filled the cabin; every evening there would be a skillet bubbling on the fire or a Dutch oven ready to be opened. But that night there was nothing. Tillman remembered a stab of annoyance. After miles of range

73

riding, he was beat and the welcome he expected wasn't there. The judge winkled that out of him in court, got him to admit that he was irritated with his wife that evening. Not enough to shoot her, but added to the other circumstances, it was one more thing. Tillman felt ashamed that fatigue had made his temper short, embarrassed that his first thought hadn't been to worry why June wasn't there.

After he was done calling out Tillman searched the land inside the junipers and discovered the old cow pony was missing. Figuring June must be over at the ranch, he climbed up on his horse again. By now, he was worried. He tried to explain this to the judge but, having admitted to being annoyed, it sounded like an excuse.

The dying light was too poor to make out tracks in the dirt. In the west, the sunset settled behind the horizon in an explosion of gold and blood-red as Tillman picked his way down the trail to the ford. In his jail cell he had relived this journey a hundred times. He remembered the slow pace of his tired horse and he recalled the cold blade of worry as he failed to figure out why June wasn't at home. He pictured darkness stalking across the sky from the east, the last defiant rage of daylight in the west. When he reached the bottom of the incline and got to the ford itself, he would have ridden straight over the body if his horse hadn't shied.

'I didn't kill her,' Tillman said.

'Prove it.' Meckets turned towards him. 'If you can't do that, why should I believe you? Why should anyone?'

Tillman stared out over the valley and said nothing. Doubts crowded in and pushed at his self-belief. He should have run; he should have headed north and found a California wagon train that needed another pair of hands. How could he have imagined that anyone back here would take his side?

In the ford, June's body had been face down. At first he mistook the blood for shadows in the water. He leapt out of his saddle, stumbled through the stream, his boots slipping. He heard himself shout at her to get up. What did she think she was doing? Get up. Get up. When he got to her panic clawed at him as he lifted her out of the water. As he turned her over in his arms and her head lolled back the strength went out of his legs. He stumbled, fought to keep himself upright and held her to him. Her body was limp; her arms fell unnaturally. His first thought was that she had fallen and broken her neck. It was only after he staggered to the edge of the stream and laid her gently down that he saw the blood on her shirt.

Tillman remembered sitting in the shadows holding June's cold hand while the remains of daylight died. The hollow chant of the stream as it ran over the stony bed was like a lament. He lost track of time. Much later he found the strength to lever himself to his feet, gather up June's body and head on up to the ranch. He remembered feeling disorientated by the blackness that surrounded him, the dead weight of the lifeless body in his arms, the monotonous thud of his horse's slow hoofbeats.

In the effort to figure out what had happened Tillman's thoughts splintered. Who could possibly have wanted to do this unthinkable thing? A robbery was out of the question: June had nothing to steal. The idea of a grudge was ridiculous: no one bore her any ill-will. An argument gone wrong was impossible: she treated everyone with fairness. An accident? Who could shoot a woman in the chest a mile from her own home by accident? And anyway, there was no one about. This was empty land. The cabin was on the east ridge, the ranch house on the west. Between them, a couple of miles south, were a few hands watching over the herd. Tillman himself had seen them from his vantage point on the high ground.

The thought in his head was that he had to tell someone, in particular he had to break the news to Meckets. That was why he headed for the ranch and not back to the cabin. All the way, grief cried out in his head. He held her body tight to him and steadied himself by gripping the edge of the saddle, barely trusting himself not to fall.

'We got company,' Meckets said suddenly.

On the road leading from the ranch house down to the ford, horses kicked up a dust cloud. Tillman shaded his eyes. The cloud was too far away for him to say how many riders there were.

'Judge's posse?' Meckets said. 'Or is it Harlan? Either way, that .45 in your hand ain't enough to save you.'

7

Both men kept their eyes on the dust cloud which moved along the ranch road. An hour, Tillman thought, at the outside.

'Look.' Meckets pointed.

Travelling up from the south was a second cloud; they hadn't noticed it before because this was where the dust kicked up by the herd hung in the air.

'Looks like you've got some of the hands after you,' Meckets said. 'Judge must have put a price on your head.'

Tillman's throat was dry. Two posses. It would be a race to see which one got to him first.

'I didn't kill her,' he said. His voice was a whisper. 'I told you.'

'Expect me to believe that?' Meckets snarled. 'You turned up at my door with my daughter's dead body in your arms in the middle of the night. She had two slugs in her chest. When the sheriff checked the chamber of your .45, how many slugs was missing?'

'That don't prove nothing. I told you I—'

Meckets's face was the colour of bone.

'Two,' he snapped.

When Tillman answered his voice was leaden.

'I shot a rabbit. I brought it home. I told everyone a thousand times.'

Meckets turned away as if he couldn't stand even to look at Tillman.

'Who shoots rabbits with a .45? And when I got up to your place where was this rabbit?' His voice was bitter. 'Oh, you told the judge it was a few days before. Couldn't be more convenient.'

'I leave the shotgun at home.' Tillman went through it again. 'June gets nervous if there ain't no gun in the house. I was riding home and this cottontail jumped out in front of me. Took a couple of shots and hit him with the second.'

He stared at Meckets.

'June put him in the pot that night. Of course you couldn't find any sign of him, you know how she cleans up. . . .'

Tillman's words dried; this was pointless. Meckets had made up his mind not to believe him. He turned his attention to the dust clouds, one inching along the ranch road, the other moving up parallel with the stream. It was a race between his executioners. The cow hands would call for a lynching; the Governor's posse wouldn't want the bother of taking him back to jail. Fear turned a blade in his guts. Even though he knew the hands well, he couldn't count on anyone to step up for him. The words *I didn't kill her* screamed in his head. He fought against the instinct to run. If he took off now, he would only have an hour's start; they would catch him before the end of the day and understand it as an admission of guilt. He had to stand firm.

'June came over early in the afternoon,' Meckets said. 'Ran right up on to the porch, tears flooding down her face. Wouldn't tell me what the matter was until I kept on at her. Eventually she couldn't keep it in no longer. Said you'd told her Harlan was cutting the herd and you'd gone up on to the ridge to spy on him.'

Meckets turned towards him. His face was pale.

'You were making accusations about my nephew and the first person you told was June.'

'I wanted to warn her.' Tillman's voice was quiet and firm. 'I knew it was him. I just had to make sure.'

'And did you?' Meckets snarled. 'You spent all day up on the ridge. Did you make sure?'

'I could see it was him; I couldn't make out the others,' Tillman said quietly. 'I told the judge.'

'June was distraught,' Meckets went on. 'Said you told her he'd been cutting the herd all season. She said you were going after him. She didn't know what you were going to do.'

'I was angry,' Tillman said. 'Harlan was cheating all of us. I helped to build up that herd. I told her I was going to get the proof I needed. She knew I wouldn't do nothing without that.'

Tillman stared out at the dust cloud again and tried to work out how far it had moved along the ranch road. All he knew was that the posse would be here before the riders from the herd.

'You're covering for him,' Tillman poured salt on an open wound. 'Your own nephew was stealing from you. You can't face that.'

Meckets launched himself at Tillman, fists swinging. He was a big bear of a man, wild with fury. Tillman ratcheted back the hammer of his .45, jabbed it into Meckets's throat and brought him up short. He planted a boot in his chest and shoved him sprawling backwards.

'You rode out to the herd,' Tillman said. 'What did Harlan say?'

Meckets eased himself up so that he was leaning back against one of the junipers again.

'Hell with you. I don't know what you're talking about.'

He stared across the valley. 'Why don't you run?' His words were sour with contempt. 'I'd like to see those boys ride you down.'

'You took off from the ranch and headed straight for the herd,' Tillman persisted. 'I saw you. What did Harlan say when you got there?'

'You're crazy,' Meckets said. 'You been in that jail cell too long. I don't know why they didn't put a noose around your neck the day they took you there and have done with it.'

'I wrote an appeal for clemency,' Tillman said. 'That's why.'

Meckets laughed. 'And the Governor turned you down.'

'Letter said "without further justification by way of evidential support from the ranch owner, the plea for clemency was dismissed",' Tillman said. 'You put the noose around my neck.'

'Best thing I ever done.' Meckets glared at him.

'That afternoon,' wearily, Tillman began again, 'you rode out from the ranch. South towards the herd.'

Meckets glared at him. Why was Tillman still bellyaching about something that wasn't true? What difference was it going to make?

'Hell I did.'

'I saw you.'

Meckets sighed, stared out into the desert and tried to compare the progress of the cloud on the ranch road with the dust kicked up by riders from the south.

'I'm sick of this,' Meckets said. 'You're a dead man.'

'I saw you ride out of the ranch and head south.' Tillman refused to give up. 'Late afternoon. I was up on the ridge.'

'I stayed in the ranch house with June,' Meckets thundered. 'She was upset. You'd tried to turn her against her own kin and it didn't work. I stayed with her till she went home. I tried to get her to stay, I don't mind telling you. Last person I wanted my daughter to be with right then was you.'

'I can prove it,' Tillman said.

'I've known guys argue night was day,' Meckets snapped. 'What are you talking about?'

'It's on the drawing. I was up on the ridge. I drew the herd, the whole valley. It shows the herd being cut and driven towards Stealer's. I was going to use it as proof to show you.'

Meckets' face was carved out of rock.

'It shows you riding south from the ranch,' Tillman went on.

'How many more times? I stayed in the house with June.' Meckets said. 'I was doing accounts all day, even after she went home.'

'I can show you,' Tillman said.

He shoved himself to his feet.

'Sketch book is in the cabin.'

'You and your damn drawings,' Meckets said. 'That don't prove nothing. You can draw anything any time.'

'I've been in jail,' Tillman snapped. 'The drawings were here, where I left them.'

With Meckets's gun shoved in his belt, he pushed through the brush between the trees. He couldn't tell if

Meckets was lying or if the distress of seeing June that day made him forget about riding out to the herd.

'Better hurry up,' Meckets called after him. 'Posse ain't slowing down.'

Concentrating on trying to convince Meckets made Tillman forget about Ludza. As soon as he cut through the line of trees, he remembered. He expected to see the guard's skinny body slumped in the cabin doorway. But he was gone.

With a glance to left and right, Tillman levelled his .45 at the open doorway and slowed his pace as he crossed the yard. No movement inside the cabin; no sound. Ludza could be waiting to jump him when he set foot inside. Just to be sure, Tillman skirted the building and peered in through the window. No one. He scanned the trees again. Nothing. Ludza must have high-tailed it or decided to hide out in the junipers till the posse showed.

Half-expecting the barrel of Ludza's Winchester to jab at him, Tillman caught his breath as he pushed back the cabin door. Everything was just as he'd left it, the supplies to one side of the chimney, the ashes in the grate, the bed against the far wall. Tillman retrieved his sketch book from where he had flung it. The book was face down, open at the sketch of *Getting Near Sundown*. The herd was there in the drawing; the dust kicked up by the cow hands in the south hung in the air; more important, so did a cloud kicked up by the rider heading at speed away from the ranch house. Tillman peered at the pencil marks. It had to be Meckets on his way to confront his nephew.

That had to be it. What was he bound to do the minute June told him? High-tail it south, aiming to catch Harlan red-handed. What would anyone do?

Problem was, all this added up to a pile of nothing. So

what if Meckets rode out and accused Harlan of cutting the herd; so what if Meckets was riled; so what if Harlan was burning up with fury. None of this told him who killed June. Meckets loved his daughter; surely, even at his wildest, Harlan would never harm her.

So why was Meckets denying that he rode out to accuse Harlan? He had to be covering something up. Tillman's brain cart-wheeled. He began to think the unthinkable. Maybe Harlan had got so mad, he'd ridden after June. He caught up with her. They argued. He drew his gun and shot her. Was Harlan capable of that?

Then another thought ambushed him. What if Meckets had killed her? June told him what Tillman thought Harlan was up to. Meckets defended him, as he always would. June insisted. In the argument, Meckets waved his gun around and. . . ? Could Meckets be covering for himself? Despite the gathering heat of the day, Tillman shivered. If Meckets was determined to frame him, he was dead, for sure.

There was a third possibility. What if Joe Whipple had heard the row? Meckets vouched for him being up at the ranch. What if Whipple hatched a wild spur-of-the-moment plan? Believing Tillman was out on the range somewhere, he waited for Meckets to leave the ranch, followed June home, shot her at the ford and left her body for Tillman. Payback for his pa at last. He would have been back at the ranch hours before Meckets returned; Meckets wouldn't have suspected he had been away.

If that was the case, did Meckets know? Why would he cover for him? Why did he deny riding south from the ranch? Whipple hated Tillman enough to do it. But when he swore to the judge he'd been working in the forge at the back of the ranch all afternoon, Meckets backed him up. Why would he do that if it wasn't true?

Tillman stared at the open sketch book in his hand. The whole valley was there, the two banks of hills, the river, the ranch and, in the distance, Meckets' herd. The place should have been paradise. The land was rich, the cattle were fat; it was an oasis of plenty in a hostile land. It was everything Meckets ever wanted and everything Tillman worked for. The two men had achieved what they set out to achieve, money, security, work and land. But now that they had, Meckets was left hard and bitter and Tillman was destined for the rope.

Tillman closed the sketch book and took a look around the cabin. Memories of June flooded over him again. Propped beside the empty hearth, the supplies were where she'd left them; laid across the bed was the quilt she'd spent last winter sewing. Pinned to the wooden wall were pages from Tillman's sketch books that she had taken a liking to: a portrait of the Hereford bull Meckets had bought to cross with the longhorns, a sketch of the men watering the herd, a drawing of the cabin where they lived. A voice in Tillman's head told him it was going to be the last time he would see these things.

As Tillman crossed the yard his guts turned to water again. Fear flickered in his brain and told him to run. His horse was a couple of minutes away; if he made a break for it now, he might be able to find somewhere to hole up when the posse came looking. With luck, he might be able to keep a distance from them until dark and then he could take his chances. In the desert at night, he might be able to give them the slip.

By the time Tillman reached the junipers he'd got a grip on himself. He was innocent. He had to prove it. There was no other way. He gripped the sketch book tight.

Either the drawing would jog Meckets' memory or show that he was lying. That picture was the first step along the path to proving that the judge got it wrong.

Meckets was still sitting where Tillman had left him. His back was against a juniper trunk and he was staring at the dust cloud down on the ranch road. The cloud was closer. Tillman checked the progress of the cowhands making their way up from the herd. They were closer too.

'Got the sketch book,' Tillman said.

He thumbed it open at the last drawing.

Meckets didn't even turn towards him.

'So what?'

'Look at it,' Tillman said.

He held the page open.

Meckets glanced at it and then looked up at Tillman.

'How many more times?' His voice was weary.

'Look at it,' Tillman repeated. He thrust the picture under Meckets's face.

Meckets considered it briefly.

'This shows you riding south to the herd.' Tillman pointed. 'Right there.'

'I've told you,' Meckets said. 'I didn't.'

He read the title at the bottom of the picture and looked at the date.

'Always write the date?'

He flicked back through the drawings. Each one was titled and dated in the bottom corner.

'This don't prove nothing,' Meckets said. 'I told you I didn't ride out to the herd. This is you trying to cook up some lame story. What are you trying to do, convince me someone shot June and dumped her body in the ford while I rode out?'

'Whipple was at the ranch,' Meckets said. 'Judge never

85

questioned him.'

'He never questioned him because I said he was in the forge, that's why. How did I know? I was in the ranch house with June. I never rode south that afternoon.'

'The drawing shows—' Tillman started.

'Hell with the drawing.'

Meckets shoved the sketch book aside and glared at him.

Neither of them heard Ludza step out of the brush. One moment they were alone, the next he was behind Tillman with his Bowie pressed across his windpipe.

'Toss them .45s.' Ludza's voice cracked like glass.

Tillman lobbed his guns into the brush.

Meckets levered himself up and hurried off in search of his pistol.

'What's this?' Ludza yanked the sketch book out of Tillman's hand.

'Drawings,' Tillman said.

'Reckons one of 'em proves he's innocent.' Meckets retrieved his .45 and pointed it at Tillman's belly.

Ludza kicked Tillman's legs away and sent him sprawling.

'Stay there where I can keep an eye on you.'

While Meckets covered him, Ludza leafed through the sketches.

'Why do you draw all these steers?' He looked baffled.

'Last page,' Meckets said. 'Reckons it proves he's innocent.'

'Yeah?'

Ludza leafed through until he came to the last drawing.

'Sundown at Stealer's Creek,' he intoned. 'Even got the date.'

He compared the sketch in his hand with the landscape

in front of him, looking quickly from one to the other.

'Not bad,' he said. 'Put the herd in there and every-thing.'

'Reckons it shows me riding south,' Meckets went on.

Ludza studied the sketch.

'If I was out of the way, that meant I didn't see the guy leave the ranch, follow my daughter to the ford and kill her.' Meckets waved the .45 at Tillman. 'That's what you're saying, ain't it?'

'That could have happened,' Tillman said.

'You're saying this drawing proves you're innocent?'

Ludza's smile crooked his mouth.

Tillman nodded.

'Keep him covered,' Ludza said.

He felt in his pocket for the stub of a stogie, pushed it to the side of his mouth, found a match and snicked the phosphorous with his fingernail. He drew on the cigar and breathed a cloud of blue smoke. As the match burned low he held it against the edge of Tillman's sketch book and watched flame curl across the paper.

Tillman lunged forward and made a grab. Meckets yelled. Ludza stepped quickly back out of Tillman's reach and held the book high to let the flame eat across the page. The ashes of *Getting Near Sundown at Stealer's Creek* floated to the ground like snow.

8

Meckets launched himself at Tillman and buried him like a landslide. He jabbed the barrel of the .45 into the side of his neck and elbowed his face in the dirt. Ludza stood over them and let the flakes of ash fall.

When the page was burned Meckets shifted his bulk and let Tillman up. He indicated a tree trunk where he wanted Tillman to sit. Tillman gulped in air, waited for his breathing to even out and wondered if Meckets landing on him had cracked any ribs. He stared across the valley. In the south, the cowhands were still moving, but down the ranch road the dust cloud was still.

'Posse ain't moving,' Ludza said. 'What's holding 'em up?'

'They're at the ford,' Meckets said. 'Judge is explaining to 'em this was where it happened.'

He stabbed a look at Tillman. 'Where Tillman shot my daughter.'

Ludza grinned.

'No drawing to say he didn't.'

'Drawings don't matter.' Tillman refused to give Ludza the satisfaction. 'I know what happened.'

'Hell you do,' Meckets snapped. 'I was in the ranch

house. Took me most of the afternoon to get June to spill out your wild stories. As much as I could do to stop saddling up and coming after you right then. I would have, if I hadn't promised.'

'June leave before you?' Tillman tried a different tack.

'How many more times?' Meckets thumbed back the hammer of the .45. 'I told you, I didn't leave. I stayed there. Whipple was in the forge. I heard him. That hammer tolled like a funeral bell all day. June took herself off just before dark.'

'They're moving again,' Ludza interrupted. 'About time. What have they been talking about down there?'

'Must have the sheriff with them,' Meckets said. 'That guy talks a storm. He'll be telling them all about how he made the arrest and when he heard what Tillman had to say, how he went back to the ford and looked for tracks in the mud. Signs of a struggle, he called it.'

'Find any?' Ludza's thin smile drew across his mouth.

'Nothing to find, was there?' Meckets turned to Tillman. 'Wasn't no struggle, was there? You just rode up to June and shot her right then and there in the middle of the ford. She was riding from the ranch direction; you rode from the cabin. When you met in the middle, that was it.'

Tillman stared at the column of dust inching up the ranch road. He wondered how long it would be before they could hear the sound of the hoofs.

'You got it all wrong,' Tillman said wearily. 'Everyone has.'

'Soon as the judge gets here, I'll claim the reward,' Ludza said. He looked nervously at Meckets. 'I was the one that tracked him here, right?'

'Think I care about reward money?' Meckets said. 'I just

89

want to see him swing. Harlan will say the same when he gets here.'

'What will the judge say when I tell him I paid you three hundred to spring me from jail?' Tillman stared at Ludza.

'You let him escape?' Meckets turned.

'Bull,' Ludza laughed nervously. 'He's just saying that.'

'You got three hundred in your pocket,' Tillman said flatly. 'That's the money I paid you to get me out.'

'That true?' Meckets eyed him. 'I'm standing in a snakes' nest. You two deserve each other. A killer and a lying son-of-a-bitch. I'll be surprised if the judge don't string you both up side by side.'

Ludza took a pace backwards.

'He wouldn't do that. I'm the one who's turning you in and claiming the reward fair and square. All that other stuff, that's just lies. Every prisoner claims he's innocent; the judge ain't going to believe none of that.'

'You sure?' Tillman said quietly. 'I heard the judge ain't a forgiving man.'

Ludza's smile slipped from his mouth. He looked first at Meckets then at Tillman.

'If you run now, the judge will put a price on your head.' Tillman turned the knife. 'Bet I know who will be riding after you.'

'Who's that?' Ludza's voice dried in his throat.

Tillman looked at Meckets.

'Harlan wouldn't turn down a chase if there was a reward at the end of it, would he?'

'Sure wouldn't,' Meckets said. 'Good horseman too. You wouldn't get away from him.'

Ludza's face was the colour of ash; his eyes flicked from Tillman to Meckets and back again. He stepped forward and retrieved the .45 from the brush.

'Anyone who comes after me gets a bullet,' he said. 'You tell 'em.'

He turned and crashed into the undergrowth in the direction of the cabin. A minute later Meckets and Tillman heard hoofbeats.

'Saw him off without firing a shot,' Meckets said. 'Ain't going to happen when the posse get here.'

'You know I would never harm June.' Tillman wouldn't give up. 'You believe that, don't you?'

'I believe what my eyes and ears tell me,' Meckets snapped. 'From what I saw of her that day, you two must have had some mighty argument. Reckon you was still spitting nails when you came home. She wasn't there, so you went looking for her. When you found her down at the ford you knew she'd been spilling all her trouble over at the ranch; that made you mad enough to draw your gun.'

'You're wrong,' Tillman said simply. 'It wasn't nothing like that.'

'I'm sick of arguing with you.' Meckets turned away. 'Just shut up and wait for the posse.'

He laid the .45 across his lap and stared out at the two dust clouds.

Neither man spoke. The sky was pale over the valley; the stream glittered in the morning light and the bank of foothills on each side protected the strip of fertile land like the crook of an arm. Higher up the slopes, the white-leaf oaks shimmered from green to pale silver as the breeze lifted their leaves. Dust hung over the herd in the south; in the west, the wooden roof of the ranch house gleamed in the sun. It was an impressive spread. Every couple of months Meckets added more out buildings: stables, stores, a forge; only the bunkhouse looked old and weather-worn. On the edge of a line of barns a skeleton of joists and roof beams was visible; this was the new feed store.

From the juniper branches, above where the men sat, came the high chip chip note of the redstarts' warning call. Tillman stared up but the birds hid themselves amongst the leaves. The birds sensed danger, a redtail circling maybe, a weasel in the brush.

Right now, with the posses closing, Tillman had this madcap idea that he should throw himself at Meckets, kick the .45 out of his hand and run. He could make it to his horse and be away before either posse got here. He had to do something; he couldn't just sit here and wait for the rope. He had come back to prove his innocence. In the back of his mind, he held on to the idea that he would be able to get through to Meckets, rekindle some old spark of friendship, rely on the fact that Meckets knew what June meant to him.

There was no chance; Meckets stonewalled. Dealing with Ludza's threats and lies had been easy; Meckets didn't want to know. To distract himself from the panic which rose inside him, Tillman grabbed a handful of dirt and watched it slip through his fingers while he struggled to arrange his thoughts in straight lines.

'You saw that drawing,' Tillman began. 'Who was riding south if it wasn't you?'

'Don't you ever quit?' Meckets sneered. 'You could have put that in the drawing at any time.'

'But I didn't,' Tillman said.

'Say what you like,' Meckets said. 'It don't prove nothing. The judge—'

'The judge wouldn't even look at it,' Tillman said. 'He wasn't interested in justice, he just wanted to stamp his authority. He rides in twice a year, makes sure he hangs whoever's in the dock at the time and rides out. That way he makes everyone afraid of the law. What kind of judge won't look at the evidence and refuses to let a defendant speak?'

'This is hard country,' Meckets admitted. 'You've gunned down rustlers, you know that.'

'Rustlers I went after were guilty,' Tillman said quickly. 'And I caught 'em red handed. That's why I went up on the ridge that day. I wasn't about to accuse Harlan without proof.'

Meckets stared out at the dust cloud. The posse slowed as they started to make the climb.

'If it wasn't you and it wasn't Whipple who rode south that afternoon, there was only one person it could have been.' Tillman's voice was calm as though he was explaining the details of how to load a gun to someone who had never held one before.

'You're saying it was June?' Meckets said.

'She could have rode out to the herd to confront Harlan.'

'She told me she was headed home,' Meckets insisted. 'It was getting dark. Would have been pitch by the time she'd got to the herd.'

'Facing down Harlan is the kind of thing she'd do,' Tillman said. 'I should have thought of that before I told her.'

'First you don't know who shot her, then you're saying it was Whipple, now you're implying Harlan shot his own cousin?' Meckets shook his head. 'Sounds like a river of lies and you're drowning in it.'

'It's possible though, ain't it?'

'No,' Meckets exploded. 'It ain't. How can you even

think that? We all rode here from Texas to make a new life. She was his cousin.'

'Could have been an accident,' Tillman persisted.

'Trying to tell me that Harlan thought she was somebody else?'

'It was getting dark.'

'Dark or light,' Meckets thundered. 'Of course he would have known it was her.'

Above his head, the redstarts burst through the greenery in an attempt to get away. The men looked up and saw the blood-red flash amongst the leaves. Meckets picked up the .45 and pointed it at Tillman.

'First you make one accusation then you make another. Throw all the dirt you want, none of it ain't gonna stick.'

'These ain't wild accusations,' Tillman said quietly.

'For a start, the herd is in the opposite direction to the ford. You're saying, if it wasn't Whipple who trailed June to the ford, it was Harlan who tracked her? That jail cell has turned your brain to mush.'

Exasperated, Meckets waved the gun.

'Anyway, what about the tracks? The sheriff went over the ground early next morning.'

'Didn't find any,' Tillman said.

'That's right. If Harlan had followed June, there would have been some kind of a scuffle at the ford, same if Whipple had followed her. Instead there was nothing. That means that there wasn't no scuffle. That means they didn't follow her.'

Gun in hand, Meckets shoved himself to his feet. He strode out of the shade of the trees to get a better view of the road up from the ranch.

'I don't know why I'm wasting my breath. Why is that posse taking so long?'

94

'That still don't mean—' Tillman persisted.

'Another thing,' Meckets said. 'My daughter's killer shot her in the chest. He was looking her in the eye. He rode up to her in the middle of the ford and shot her. He wasn't chasing her, he wasn't following after her, he stood right there in front of her and shot her dead. And that was you, Tillman. You can forget all your lies and excuses and trying to pin the blame. That was you, convicted by a judge in a court of law. You may have escaped once but I'm going to see your neck break for it.'

As Tillman stared out into the valley something panicked the redstarts; they hopped from branch to branch as if they wanted to escape but they didn't know where the danger was. A second later he heard the rumble of the hoofs on the ranch road. Meckets heard it too. They both turned to where the road entered the yard out on the other side of the trees.

'I'm innocent,' Tillman said. 'I didn't run. I came back here to prove it.'

Meckets held the .45 steady.

'Don't you try anything.' He took a pace back into the brush. 'Won't be long now.'

Tillman calculated the distance between him and Meckets. He might be able to jump him, but not before Meckets got off a shot. If he ran now, it would be with a gutful of lead. Nevertheless, he fought down his instinct to high-tail it into the brush. Maybe someone in the posse would listen to him, maybe the judge would give him the benefit of the doubt. Maybe a miracle would happen and they would all believe him and let him go. Every second, the sound of the hoofs was louder.

It was hopeless. Tillman knew it. It was too late to run, even if he wanted to. If Meckets didn't believe him, why should the judge? All that was going to happen was they would haul him back to jail and stand him on the gallows trapdoor. He was a prisoner who had bribed a guard to let him escape. No more, no less. It was too late for whys and wherefores. No one was interested.

In his head, the sound of the hoofbeats took Tillman back to the night he found June. He had left the cabin angry and fearful. Angry because, that morning when he had told her his suspicions about Harlan, she had flat out contradicted him. She told him he was dreaming: Harlan would never steal from his uncle who had brought him on the long ride from Texas, trusted him and built a ranch which one day he would partly own. All her life she had made excuses for Harlan; family loyalty was as natural to her as breathing. This was just one more example of how people didn't see the good in him that she saw. She would be the first to admit that Harlan wasn't easy. She knew full well he rubbed folks up the wrong way, that he was liable to get himself in trouble, that he'd argued with his pa almost since the day he was born. But it didn't make any difference: he was kin; she took his side just like she always had. Now her own husband was telling her that Harlan was cutting the herd and he was setting out that day to get proof. She would have none of it; when they parted that morning the argument between them was unresolved.

When Tillman returned home and to find a cold grate and an empty cabin, he knew something had happened, June was always there to greet him; she had never been away before. He remembered the thud of his horse's hoofs as he hurried through the gap in the junipers and down the track to the ranch.

In the dying light, looking down on the ford, something caught his eye. At first he thought it was a bed sheet; a rolled-up mattress had fallen off a wagon as it jolted over the riverbed. He recalled thinking how odd it was since no wagons ever came that way. When he got down to the edge of the stream he saw the truth. He leapt off his horse, slipped on the stones and half-fell, half-ran towards where June's body lay. Blocking out the sound of the flowing water, the blood pounded in his head as hard as hoofbeats. He picked her up and cradled her in his arms as though she was hurt and needed his tenderness. He remembered how cold her body felt, how the water streamed out of her clothes and out of her hair. Shock juddered through him when he realized she had been shot and the stain on the front of her shirt was blood. He remembered how he stumbled to the riverbank with his strength ebbing out of him and laid her gently in the dirt where the edge of the water meets the track.

The pounding in his head was loud now as he remembered how beautiful she was; he remembered staring at her for a long time until the daylight ended and darkness made it impossible for him to see her face. It was only then that he gathered her up in his arms again and headed across the stream in the direction of the ranch. Meckets, June's father, was the first person he had to tell.

The sound of horses in the yard on the other side of the junipers jolted Tillman out of his reverie. He heard the riders shout to each other. He heard the cabin door bang open. Meckets faced him with the .45 levelled at his gut; there was a cold smile across his mouth. Tillman scrambled to his feet in case the horsemen tried to ride him down and he would have to dive out of the way.

'Over here,' Meckets called. 'Other side of the trees.'

'Who's that?' a voice answered.

Tillman couldn't recognize who it was: one of the prison guards maybe or one of the sheriff's men riding point?

'Meckets. I got him. He's right here.'

Meckets steadied the gun at Tillman's chest.

'He armed?' the voice queried. 'I don't want to get shot at.'

Tillman knew the voice; he just couldn't place it.

'He ain't armed,' Meckets called back. 'I got a gun on him.'

He turned to Tillman.

'Just you stand there and don't move. Don't you try anything at all.'

There were voices on the other side of the junipers.

'Quickest if you dismount,' Meckets called into the trees. 'Leave your horses in the yard, you won't get 'em through the brush.'

The man called an acknowledgement. Tillman could hear voices discuss the best place to tether the horses. Then he heard the crash of footsteps as the riders found a way between the trunks of the junipers. He heard their voices as they called out directions to each other about the best path to take. He heard them curse as, in their haste, the briers snagged their clothes.

Meckets caught his breath, took a pace backwards and clenched his fists by his sides. A second later the first man broke through the undergrowth and stepped through the line of trees. He was tall, lean and blond-haired with a fat nicotined moustache hanging over his mouth like a yard broom. He wore a black hat and jacket, a white shirt with no collar and a pair of silver Colts in tooled leather holsters at his hip. When he saw the two men, his face creased into an easy smile.

'Hi there, Tillman,' he said. 'How the hell did you get yourself into this mess?'

9

'Reverend Bullhorn?' Meckets' jaw dropped: he recognized the stranger too.

'Holster that sidearm, friend,' Bullhorn said. 'No call for weapons.'

'Where's the judge?' Meckets snapped. 'I'm holding this man prisoner.'

Meckets held his gun levelled at Tillman.

'Judge Duval?' Bullhorn looked vague. 'Met him heading north. Said he was chasing Tillman. We agreed with him that Tillman would never come back here. Best place he could look was the Phoenix trail.'

'You sent him north?' Meckets looked stunned.

'It was a lie.' Bullhorn shrugged. 'But I figured the judge wouldn't want to hang an innocent man, so I helped him avoid doing that.'

Tillman laughed out loud.

Two women stepped out of the brush and stood behind Bullhorn. Their long hair was tied back and they wore black jackets and hats, men's collarless shirts and pants just like the reverend.

'These here's Ida and Lilly, my two angels,' Bullhorn announced. 'They assist me in my work.'

Meckets' jaw dropped.

'Found 'em in unfortunate circumstances and I saved 'em. Now they ride with me.'

Both the women moved back the edges of their jackets to reveal pearl handled Colts in black leather holsters.

'I'm asking you one more time. . . .'

Bullhorn didn't have to finish. Meckets slid his .45 back into its holster.

'Thank you,' Bullhorn said.

'You ain't said what you're doing here,' Meckets grumbled.

'I'm doing what I do everywhere.' Bullhorn sounded surprised to be asked. 'Saving souls. That's the business I'm in.'

'Thought you sold snake oil.' Meckets glowered.

'That too. Heal the body; save the soul. I left my wagon down at your ranch packed to the bonnet with my latest stock of elixirs. I got lotions for all ills. Give 'em to you at a good price. What ails you, friend?'

'I'm talking about Tillman,' Meckets snapped.

'Heard he was in trouble, so me and my angels came. You're forgetting I presided over the marriage union of Tillman here and your daughter. I ain't about to neglect someone I had dealings with in the past. I heard about the tragedy and I heard Tillman shouldered the blame.'

'Where did you hear all this?'

'Talk of a hanging travels fast through this territory. I headed straight for the jail. I know this man; I know he's innocent. I know the judge too. Reckoned he'd listen to me if I vouched for him. My angels can be mighty persuasive. More than that, I reckoned Tillman here would pay me a soul-saving fee.' He turned to Tillman. 'Three hundred would cover it.'

'This is bull,' Meckets stormed. 'I aim to see Tillman hang. It won't take the judge long to figure you sent him on a fool's trail; he'll turn about by nightfall.'

'You're an angry man, Meckets,' Bullhorn said. 'I know you've endured tragedy and you're hurting because of that. You may say you want justice but what you are really hankering after is revenge. . . .'

As rage flared in his face Meckets went for his gun. But he was too slow. In the second it took him to reach for his holster, both Bullhorn's Colts were in his hands. On either side of the Reverend, the two women also had their pistols aimed at Meckets's gut.

'Reckon we'd better take that .45 off you.' Bullhorn nodded to Tillman. 'Never know when there might be an accident.'

Tillman stepped across and slid the gun out of Meckets' holster.

'Good.' Bullhorn's face creased into a smile. He and the two women holstered their weapons. 'Now, we've got some straightening out to do,' he went on. 'Before we attend to that, I need to cover expenses.' He turned to Tillman. 'About that three hundred. . . .'

'Paid it to the guard who sprung me.'

'All of it?' Bullhorn sounded hurt.

Tillman nodded.

'Would this be the fella we ran into an hour ago? He was pleased when we was able to direct him to the Governor's posse. Mentioned something about having a reward to collect.'

'That's him,' Tillman said. 'Name's Ludza.'

'Don't give a fig what his name is.' Bullhorn sounded affronted. 'You paid him three hundred for springing you out of jail and now he's intending to collect from the

102

Governor for telling him where you're at?'

'World is full of crooks, ain't it?' Meckets said sourly.

Bullhorn beamed. His eyes creased and his moustache lifted.

'See, we're all getting along just fine. I knew we would.'

'Reverend, do you want me to . . .' Ida started to speak.

'I surely do.' Bullhorn's face lit up. 'Ida don't even have to tell me and I know what she's talking about.'

'Guess that means you want me to . . .' Lilly began.

'That's right.' The reverend turned to Tillman. 'Got any supplies up here? I'm starved; straightening out is hungry work.'

'In the cabin,' Tillman said.

The two women disappeared into the brush, leaving Tillman and Meckets to stare after them.

'Ida's gone to get the three hundred off that prison guard. Lilly's gone to make us some chow,' Bullhorn explained. 'Let's sit down and take in the view, gentlemen. When we've had something to eat we'll get down to the straightening out.'

The three men sat down and leaned back against juniper trunks. Above them a pair of redstarts settled on a branch and sat still. As the morning heat built, the air twisted down in the valley and made it difficult to judge the progress of the dust column as it moved along the trail. Sometimes it seemed to indicate a whole gang of riders; other times it seemed like just a single man; sometimes it seemed as though it was an hour away, at others it seemed closer to four.

Bullhorn studied the dust cloud with interest. Struggling to hold on to his temper, Meckets divided his attention between darting looks of contemptuous loathing at the reverend and glaring down at his own boots.

Tillman leaned back, enjoyed the warm morning air on his face and listened to the high whistle of the redstarts' song, grateful for the time Bullhorn had bought him.

It was true that Bullhorn was the preacher who had married Tillman and June. Without a church building for hundreds of miles, the territory relied on travelling preachers to provide religion. Once he and June had decided to tie the knot it was simply a question of waiting for a preacher to turn up. Sure enough, one spring day Bullhorn arrived at the newly built ranch house in a covered wagon. He was on his own then, a persuasive sales-man and a loquacious sermonizer.

From the first time Bullhorn opened his mouth, Meckets disliked him. Right from the get-go, he resented seeing his ranch hands part with their pay for evil-smelling liniments to cure aches and pains which, up until then, they hadn't known they had. His first instinct was to throw the reverend off his land. But Bullhorn's gift of the gab made him popular amongst the men; he was a sideshow after the monotony of long days in the saddle. If it amused them, Meckets calculated, where was the harm? Plainly, the guy was intent on charming the dollars out of their pockets and meant to be well on his way before the extrav-agant claims he made for his medicines could be tested. ('No such thing as an instant cure,' he boasted. 'Best to lay in a few weeks' supply.') But, if the men chose to part with their hard-earned cash, it was up to them.

Tillman and June were oblivious: Bullhorn had promised to marry them. They walked on air. They hardly noticed that the reverend had mysteriously mislaid his Bible and had to borrow one from the bride's father; they couldn't have cared less that he seemed to be making up his words on the spot or that the ceremony contained an offbeat analogy between marriage and the power of healing guaranteed by the patent medicines he happened to be carrying with him. They even failed to take offence when he tried to press on them, at a reduced price, a special elixir to be taken by bride and groom on their wedding night.

In return, Bullhorn felt protective towards Tillman and his young bride. They were the first couple he had married, he told them. He was touched by the faith they put in him; he realized Tillman held back from objecting to his sales pitch so as not to spoil the day for his new wife and he was grateful. Also, sensing that both the ranch hands and the newlyweds provided a long-term potential market for his potions, he not only promised never to forget them but swore he would go out of his way to call in on them every year in case there was anything he could help them with.

Of course, Meckets hadn't reckoned on June announcing that she and Tillman had arranged for the reverend to marry them before he headed out. Once again, he bit the bullet. By then, he had pretty much come to terms with the fact that Tillman had stolen June's heart and had worked out his plan for keeping them close by letting them have the cabin. Now, it was just a question of making himself appear delighted when the day came. He took comfort in the sure knowledge that he wasn't the first father who had to do this and, sure as hell, wouldn't be the last.

Meckets also had to keep his eye on Harlan, whose jealousy was palpable. Then there was eighteen-year-old Joe Whipple whose loathing for Tillman had run so deep since the accident that Meckets was surprised he hadn't jacked in his job and headed off to Tuscon. Meckets prided himself on his ability to steer his employees through these stormy seas as well as keeping a firm hand on day-to-day business. His ability to do this at the same time as keeping a weather eye on his long-term profit margins, he told himself, was why he was boss and they weren't.

Now Meckets's world had stopped turning. His beloved daughter was dead. A judge had ruled that her own husband, the man Meckets used to trust above anyone else, had killed her. It looked like Harlan's distrust of Tillman was justified. Meckets should never have let the wedding go ahead. And just as he was about to hand Tillman back to the authorities, this charlatan preacher turned up out of nowhere and took Tillman's side. Right now, Meckets was certain of two things: he should have put a bullet between Tillman's eyes the night he carried June's body into the ranch house and he should have run Bullhorn off his land the first time he set eyes him.

As far as Bullhorn was concerned, he had surprised himself. Fully aware that there was little chance of him selling more than a few bottles of patent, he had turned tail and headed down here as soon as he heard what had happened. Usually, he prided himself on his business acumen and making this long journey for a negligible return was one of those rare occasions where he let his heart rule his head. His angels thought all the more of him, of course, so maybe he could factor that into his return. On the way down he had entertained them with stories about Tillman and June's wedding. Colourful as these tales were, they barely skirted the truth. In Bullhorn's version, he waived his fee and gave away a bottle of Special, his most expensive cure-all, to each of the guests. In reality, he charged Meckets double for performing the ceremony in order to cover the cost of selling bottles of Special at a percentage reduction. The angels, who were already prepared to walk over hot coals for Bullhorn, hung on his every word.

Two months previously, Bullhorn doctored a bottle of his own patent and encouraged the owner of the bordello where the two women were held prisoner to drink it down in one go. The attack of the gut gripes which followed was so severe that the bordello owner lay folded in a foetal position, bilious, sweating and crying for his mother, for the rest of the day. Shortly after flavouring a second bottle with sugar syrup, telling the owner it was honey water and coaxing him to swallow it for his own good, Ida and Lilly slipped out of the building, climbed aboard the reverend's wagon and the three of them high tailed it out of town.

'And who might that be?' Bullhorn pointed in the direction of the dust cloud.

The riders had got as far as the ranch.

'Harlan,' Meckets said. 'He's bringing up some of the boys from the herd.'

'I remember him from the wedding,' Bullhorn said. 'Took his sidearm off him when he got drunk.'

'He didn't mean no harm,' Meckets said. 'He was celebrating. The whiskey got the better of him, that's all.'

'Who comes to a wedding wearing a gun?' Bullhorn said. 'A guy with something to prove, that's who.'

Meckets refused to catch the preacher's eye; he stared fiercely at his boots.

'Don't matter now,' Tillman intervened. 'That's all in the past.'

'Hell it don't,' Meckets said. 'Harlan pleaded with me not to let you marry June. I should have listened to him.'

'Drop it,' Tillman said. 'It's in the past.'

'If I'd have listened to him, June might be alive now.'

'I've told you a million times—' Tillman began angrily.

'Woah, fellas!' Bullhorn sounded genuinely dismayed. 'This ain't "straightening out"; this is just slanging at each other for the sake of it. Just cut it out until we've all had something to eat, then we'll get down to business.'

'When Harlan and the boys get here,' Meckets glared at Tillman, 'they're gonna hogtie you and hand you over to the judge. And I'm gonna ride up to the prison to watch you hang.'

The men turned, distracted by noise in the brush behind them. Lilly pushed her way through the branches, proudly bearing a barrel lid heaped with hot Johnny cakes. The smell of baked cornmeal was mouth-watering. She had left her jacket in the cabin and rolled up her sleeves, but she still wore the Colt at her hip.

'My mama used to make these with milk and bacon fat,' she explained. 'But we only got salt and water, so that had to do.'

Suddenly gripped by a hunger they had not known they possessed, the three men made a dive for the cakes. The yellow cornmeal broke open and steamed in their hands as they scooped the cakes off the board.

'My folks were from New England originally,' Lilly went on. 'That's where you get the best Johnny cakes. Cornmeal's ground finer back there, I reckon. 'Course, some folks like to mix an egg or two in with the meal. But that's another thing we ain't got.'

'This is fine.' Bullhorn shoved in another cake and turned to the others. 'Told you she was an angel, didn't I?'

'Met a girl from Alabama once who said she made Johnny cakes with rice,' Lilly continued. 'But I ain't never tried that. Don't sound nice to me.'

She held the barrel lid patiently while the men helped themselves.

'And once I met a fella who said to bring out the best in a Johnny cake you had to pour syrup on it. I ain't never tried that neither,' she reflected. 'But I'd surely like to.'

'Don't need syrup,' Bullhorn insisted, making a grab for the last one. 'Don't need nothing. These are some of the best Johnny cakes I ever tasted. That's a fact.'

'Very good,' Tillman agreed. 'Thank you kindly.'

'Good,' Meckets mumbled appreciatively with his mouth full. 'Thank you.'

Relishing the compliments, Lilly beamed. A blush came to her pale cheek. She thanked them modestly.

'Good thing you liked 'em,' Bullhorn confided after Lilly headed back to the cabin. 'I once saw her shoot a man who complained about her cooking. She made Johnny cakes that time too.'

Tillman and Meckets stared at him.

'She don't take criticism well,' Bullhorn explained. 'Especially from men. That's because of the life she was forced to lead before I freed her.'

'Shot him dead?' Meckets sounded nervous.

'In the thigh,' Bullhorn said. 'Only a flesh wound. Said she'd shoot him in the other one if he didn't say something nice.'

'I guess he didn't waste time doing that,' Meckets said.

'Swore blind he'd made a mistake and they were the best Johnny cakes he'd ever tasted. Funny thing was,' Bullhorn went on, 'That evening she remembered she'd forgotten to put in the salt.'

109

'Too late to apologize by then, of course,' Meckets added drily.

'Packed up the wagon real quick and hit the trail after dark,' Bullhorn said. 'Always the best way.'

As the men contemplated the story, they stared across the valley. The column of dust kicked up by the hands had moved past the ranch. Under an hour, Tillman thought.

'Now we got full bellies,' Bullhorn said, 'time to get down to the straightening-out.'

'Something's burning down there.' Meckets shaded his eyes with his hand.

As they looked, close to the ranch house, thin lines of black smoke rose in the morning air.

'Is that a barn?' Tillman said.

As they watched, the smoke swelled like a chimney fire. The men stared hard, trying to make it out.

'That's my wagon,' Bullhorn yelled. 'Some sonofabitch has set light to my wagon.'

10

'The cow hands did that?' Bullhorn stared. Words dried up in his mouth.

As the dust cloud moved with the riders towards the ford, the fire took hold. A column of black smoke reached through fingers of flame and up into the sky.

'Harlan told you at the wedding he never wanted to see you here again,' Meckets said. 'Looks like he meant it.'

'He was drunk and about to cause trouble,' Bullhorn said. 'Anyone would have taken his gun off him.'

'You knocked him down in the dirt in front of the whole crowd,' Meckets said. 'He ain't forgiven you for that.'

Lilly came charging between the trees.

'Seen the fire, Reverend?' She caught her breath. 'Someone's set light to the wagon.'

'Seen it,' Bullhorn snapped.

'Want me to ride down there to check what's going on?'

Bullhorn hesitated.

'I don't want no gunplay, at least not until we have to.'

'Come on, Reverend.' Lilly grinned. 'You know me better than that.'

'You can ride down there and see how many there are.'

Bullhorn sounded doubtful. 'Just keep your gun in its holster.'

Lilly's face lit up. Without hesitation she darted back between the trees.

'If I hadn't let her go, she would have slipped away anyway,' Bullhorn reflected. 'Means well, but there are only two things she really likes doing, baking and shooting.'

'Reckon she'll get the better of Harlan?' Meckets laughed.

'Just see how many there are and report back here,' Bullhorn called.

They heard the sound of hoofs from the other side of the junipers.

Bullhorn sat down again and faced the men.

'High-tailed it down here soon as I learned Tillman was in line for a hanging.' He looked first at Tillman, then Meckets. 'Figured something had to be wrong. This fella could never shoot his own wife. I would have stood in front of the judge and said so if anybody asked me.'

'You don't know nothing,' Meckets snapped. 'There's evidence which says he shot her. The judge heard it and he passed the verdict.'

'What evidence?'

Meckets again told the story of how Tillman had turned up at the ranch house after dark with June's body in his arms. Tillman stared out at the dust cloud moving along the ranch road and let him speak.

'Don't add up.' Bullhorn dug his heels in. 'Who else could have done it?'

'You mean, just because you saw them on their wedding day they weren't capable of a falling out?'

'That's right,' Bullhorn said. 'I don't believe it. There

112

must be someone else. What about this fella working in the forge? You said he had some beef against Tillman.'

'He never left the forge. I heard him out there till way after dark,' Meckets snapped. 'Just like I never left the ranch house when June rode home. We've been over this.'

'I saw someone ride south from the ranch just before sundown,' Tillman interrupted. 'Must have been Meckets, since he's so insistent Joe Whipple stayed in the forge. It's on a sketch I did of the valley from up on the ridge.'

Meckets turned away in contempt. He studied the progress of the dust cloud.

'All right, June left the ranch and headed home.' Weary with explaining this, Tillman summoned his energy one more time. 'Meckets rode down to the herd. While he was away Whipple followed June till he caught up with her at the ford.'

'See how he's trying to weasel his way out?' Meckets thundered. 'First he's saying I rode out, then he's saying Whipple rode out. Just too convenient, ain't it? Are you surprised the judge didn't believe him?' Meckets looked Bullhorn straight in the face. 'I was in the ranch house. I spent the afternoon comforting June. She was crying and carrying on; she couldn't stand the idea that her own husband was accusing Harlan of cutting the herd. When she left, I opened the whiskey bottle, I can tell you. I didn't go nowhere.'

'Wait a minute,' Bullhorn said. 'June was shot in the chest, right?'

Meckets turned away.

'So whoever was riding after her would have had to wheel round in front of her, or she must have turned. Didn't the sheriff find any tracks at the ford?'

'Nothing,' Meckets said. 'And what does that point to?

Tillman riding towards her, down from the cabin. When he met her face on at the ford, he shot her.'

Tillman shook his head and avoided catching Meckets' eye.

'Listen, mister.' Meckets leaned towards Bullhorn as if he wanted to share a confidence. 'Harlan and his boys will be here soon. You better skedaddle if you want to avoid a bloodbath. You can quit worrying about Tillman too; the judge's posse will be here by sundown.'

'What about this drawing?' Bullhorn ignored him. 'You said it shows someone riding out from the ranch. That's evidence to back up your story if you show it to the judge.'

'Was,' Tillman said. 'Ludza held a match to it. He can't claim a reward for an innocent man.'

'Wasn't hardly proof,' Meckets sneered.

'Enough to raise a doubt, maybe?' Bullhorn said.

The dust cloud stopped moving close to the ford. Maybe the men were taking time to water their horses, Tillman thought. In spite of Bullhorn's good intentions, nothing had changed. Meckets was sure he was lying; Harlan was burning up with rage; the judge would have him in irons by nightfall. He had pinned his hopes on his sketch as a way of convincing Meckets and now that was gone.

'Let's just say,' Bullhorn began again, 'that Tillman ain't lying.' He turned confidentially to Meckets. 'You trusted him in the past; never had a reason to doubt him, did you?'

'Till now,' Meckets said.

'Let's just say he's mistaken. Maybe he truly believes you rode out from the ranch that evening.'

'Facts is facts,' Meckets snarled. 'Tracks show there was no struggle at the ford; I didn't ride out of the ranch and

114

nor did Whipple; June was upset because of what Tillman had said. He says he rode down to the ford looking for her. All this tells me he rode down looking to continue the argument; when he found her it must have got out of hand. Wouldn't be the first time he's shot an innocent man.'

The dust cloud was past the ford now and began to follow the riders up the incline to the cabin. Smoke from the burning wagon thinned to a few black lines.

'You shot someone?' Bullhorn turned to Tillman.

'Everyone knows he's quick with a gun,' Meckets said. 'Sometimes he's too quick.'

'I shot one of the ranch hands.' Tillman stared at the ground. 'It was an accident.'

'Whipple's father,' Meckets said. 'Out by the barn.'

'Came across someone breaking into the stables,' Tillman explained. 'We'd been having trouble with rustlers so we'd put padlocks on the door. After dark, one night, I came across a guy levering the locks off. Took him for a horse thief. Who wouldn't?'

'Shot him dead as a nail,' Meckets said.

'Called out to him three times,' Tillman said. 'He heard me all right, yelled at me to get the hell away. Just carried on crowbarring the lock. There was someone else with him. Turned out it was his kid.'

'Old Frank Whipple had been on the bottle all day and took it into his head to take his boy out for a night ride,' Meckets said. 'He was used up; everyone knew that. Been around ranches too long; never had a good word to say for no one. He wasn't no use as a cattle hand; I had him doing odd jobs round the place. Wasn't even much good at that.'

'What about the boy?'

'Said his pa was going to show him a way to get rich,'

Tillman said. 'Must have been going to take him down to Stealer's Creek. The kid didn't understand what he meant. Nor did we, back then.'

'We didn't know what he was talking about and we didn't have proof of nothing,' Meckets said. 'The kid was sixteen. I took him in. He lived with me and Harlan in the ranch house.'

'I quit right then and there. Didn't want no part in running the ranch after that,' Tillman said. 'Meckets bought me out of the business for three hundred cash. I took on the job of stock detective and moved out to the cabin.'

'This kid is Harlan's sidekick now?' Bullhorn asked.

'Eighteen years old now,' Meckets said. 'Can be wild, like all young fellas at that age. Rides with Harlan when they're out with the herd. Looks up to him, I guess.'

'Does he go along with cutting the herd?'

'No proof of it,' Tillman said. 'We've seen off rustlers from all over, guys from Texas, Mexicans from across the border, hands from the neighbour's ranch sometimes. Never suspected our own fellas stole from us till now.'

'You ain't never had proof,' Meckets snapped. 'And you still ain't got none. One thing's for sure, you and Harlan never got along. Now you accuse him of cutting the herd and just look what it's led to.'

A breeze got up and shifted the juniper branches above them; the quiet sigh of the leaves sounded like a deck of cards falling from a dealer's hand. The redstarts were either still and sheltering from the rising temperature or had flown off somewhere. The heat of the day climbed over the valley and twisted the air, so the view of the ranch and the river was bent out of true; what had been a perfect pastoral scene an hour before became so disfigured it was

116

hard to make out where things lay. Followed by their dust cloud, the riders wound their way up the ranch road; for a time they were out of sight from where the men sat.

Two shots from a .45 sang out in quick succession. Bullhorn jumped to his feet.

'How far away was that?'

The men strained their ears waiting for a third shot, but none came. After a while they could hear the faint sound of horses' hoofs.

Three riders, Tillman calculated. Their pace was slow, the shooting had made them cautious. He checked the chamber of his .45. His face drawn with worry, Bullhorn began to pace up and down along the edge of the junipers. Every now and then he would raise his head and listen to the sound of the hoofbeats. Only Meckets sat still. As he watched the other two, a smirk played over his mouth.

'Maybe you're all telling the truth.' Bullhorn turned to Meckets. 'You stayed in the ranch house and uncorked the whiskey; Whipple worked on in the forge; Tillman saw someone ride out of the ranch house that night. Question is, who did he see?'

'June was the only other person there.' When he realized what Bullhorn was driving at, anger darkened Meckets's face like a bruise. 'You saying she rode south to the herd? Baloney. She told me herself she was heading home.'

'Maybe she wanted to confront her cousin,' Bullhorn said.

'Damn right she wanted to.' Meckets glared at Tillman. 'This husband of hers got her so wound up she wanted to ride straight down there. I wouldn't let her. You go flinging accusations like that at Harlan, nobody ain't going to be able to rein him in. I knew if I let her do that Harlan would ride straight out, find Tillman and pump him full of lead. I persuaded her to go home. I told her, do nothing. Said I'd be the one who spoke to Harlan. If Tillman came up with any evidence, I'd confront Harlan with it.'

On the other side of the junipers the men heard a horse walk uncertainly into the yard.

'Lilly,' Bullhorn called. 'That you?'

No answer. The men listened to the sound of the horse wandering aimlessly.

'Sounds like it ain't got a rider,' Tillman said.

'Keep him covered.' Bullhorn indicated Meckets. 'I'll take a look.'

As he pushed his way into the brush Tillman drew his .45.

A couple of minutes later there was a shout from Bullhorn. Tillman gestured Meckets to head between the trees back to the yard while he followed. When they got there the reverend was struggling to lift Lilly down from the saddle. Her eyes were closed, her face was chalk and the front of her shirt was soaked in blood. Tillman rushed to help. Together they carried the lifeless body into the cabin. The place was warm from the fire and smelled of fresh baking.

'I should never have . . .' Bullhorn choked on his words; tears welled in his eyes.

'She would have gone anyway,' Tillman said. 'You said so yourself.'

It took a minute for Bullhorn to lay Lilly's body on the bed, long enough for Meckets to slip away. When they looked for him the yard was empty.

Gun in hand, half-expecting Harlan to be waiting for

118

him, Tillman stormed across the yard in the direction of the track down to the ford. Meckets must have gone to meet up with his nephew. Aiming to skirt round behind, Bullhorn headed into the trees, back towards where they had been sitting.

Tillman hesitated at the gap between the junipers where the track from the cabin widened and led down the hillside. There was a clear view from here down to the first bend. Overhung with juniper branches, the brush was thick and grew close to the trail edge. The wandering tracks of Lilly's pony were stamped in the dust.

Tillman scanned the brush. A slight breeze shifted the topmost branches of the junipers but below them nothing moved. He strained his ears to hear the tread of a horse. Silence. He glanced behind him back into the yard. Something felt wrong. Tillman struggled to figure what it was. His Colt felt heavy in his hand. In his head the oiled *snick* as he thumbed back the hammer was deafening; if anyone hadn't worked out where he was, they knew now.

Tillman suspected Harlan had a Winchester pointed right at him. If he took another step out on to the road, he would be a sitting duck. He felt a bead of sweat run down the side of his face. Harlan and Whipple could be waiting for him round the corner; they could be watching him from the brush.

'Hey, Tillman.'

There was a shout from somewhere behind him. Bullhorn's voice.

'Anything?'

Harlan had to be waiting round that corner. What was his game? Meckets would have met up with him by now. He would have told them where Tillman was; they would be able to hear Bullhorn. In fact Tillman could hear the reverend moving through the brush in front of the cabin. It wasn't like him to make so much noise, Tillman thought. He wasn't an impulsive guy: he played it safe, always calculated a move ahead. Then he remembered how broken Bullhorn's face had looked as he lifted Lilly down from the saddle, how gently he had laid her on the bed in the cabin and how he seemed mesmerized by the bright blood on her shirt.

Tillman stared down the empty track. He checked the brush on either side, looking for the slightest telltale sign: a broken branch, trampled leaves, anything.

Bullhorn called again.

'Hey, Tillman.'

If he answered he would give himself away for sure.

'Tillman, you OK?'

Worry echoed in Bullhorn's voice. With one of his angels dead, his nerve had gone.

Straight ahead, the empty track disappeared round the first of the bends which took it down the hillside to the ford. If Tillman looked hard he could see a veil of dust in the air. Whether it hung over the place where the riders had reined in their horses, or whether the breeze had carried it from further down the slope, he couldn't say. But round the other side of that first bend was the place Harlan and his boys had to be, Tillman was certain.

Thirty yards of dusty track, that was how far it was. Then it occurred to Tillman that if Harlan wanted to shoot him, he would have done it by now. Wouldn't he have thundered round the corner and ridden him down? This was some kind of waiting game. Who's going to move first? Who's got the guts to step out into the open?

After a last glance back towards the yard Tillman began to walk slowly forward. He trod lightly; tiny pillows of dust exploded round the edges of his boots. He kept his eyes dead ahead and his .45 trained high enough for a shot to knock a man out of the saddle, at the exact place where the road turned. Every step, he expected a rider to swing round and blast him. Every second, he expected someone to dive out of the shadows between the trees. It would be Whipple, he decided. Harlan would hang back, wait to see how things panned out and then ride in for the kill.

Just as Tillman reached the place where a juniper branch leaned out and the track elbowed, he heard Bullhorn call again.

'Hey, Tillman.' This far away, his voice sounded frail.

Tillman didn't answer. He steadied his aim and took the final few steps to the turn in the road.

11

Nothing.

Tillman expected a wall of riders, .45s in their hands. Instead, the empty track wound its way down the hillside just as it always had. The valley spread out below. The roofs of the ranch buildings on the opposite hill reflected the sun; the stream shone as it threaded its way along the valley gutter; to the south, dust rose over the herd.

There was no sound, no jingle of a bridle, no give-away stamp of a hoof. The brush at the side of the track was still, no snapping twigs, no movement amongst the branches. Tillman wheeled round to check that no one had sneaked up behind, but nothing followed him except his own footprints in the dust. Whether it was natural caution or a sixth sense, he couldn't shake the idea that someone was watching him. He felt it.

As Tillman turned back towards the cabin, the .45 weighed in his hand, his finger was ready on the trigger. Muffled by the dust on the track, his footsteps were barely loud enough to make a mouse skitter, but to him they announced where he was like a drumbeat. He stared into the trees, checked behind him, locked his eyes on the track ahead. But there was no one, just emptiness and silence except for the breeze shuffling the leaves in the high branches.

'Hey, Tillman.' Bullhorn again. 'Where are you? Ain't run off and left me, have you?'

Worry edged his voice. He sounded weak; calling out was an effort that cost him his strength. Tillman pictured his face, bleak with shock, as he gently lifted Lilly out of her saddle.

Instead of calling a reply Tillman stood still and listened. Just past the next juniper was where the track opened out on to the yard. He glanced behind him one last time; he stared into the brush.

'Tillman,' Bullhorn called. His voice came from in front of the cabin. 'Over here.'

As Tillman rounded the corner of the cabin, someone grabbed him. Two men. One clamped his wrist and forced his gun high in the air, another levered his other arm behind him and pressed a gun to the side of his neck. A shot from Tillman's .45 ripped into the trees. Tillman crashed face down into the dirt; the full weight of both men slammed down on top of him. One of them yelled in his ear to let go of his gun; the other knelt on his neck and wrenched his arm up between his shoulders.

When Tillman released his grip on the .45, the men peeled off him. Pain seared his ribs from where they had landed on him; his arm was wrenched half out of its socket; his neck was bruised and his mouth was full of dirt. He pushed himself up.

On the cabin porch Meckets held a gun to Bullhorn's throat. The reverend's jacket was covered in yard dust, his eye was swollen shut and there was blood in his mouth; he had lost his hat somewhere. Harlan stood beside them, his Colt trained to a spot right between Tillman's eyes. The men who jumped Tillman were Joe Whipple and Flaco Perez, a Mexican hand whom Tillman had always liked. They scrambled to their feet and watched him pick himself up. Perez looked surprised, apologetic almost, as if he only now realized what his boss had told him to do. His hat had also been knocked off in the scuffle and had rolled out into the yard somewhere. Whipple glared at Tillman.

'Want me to finish him off?' Harlan appealed to Meckets. 'I could drill him right now.'

'Do it.' Whipple couldn't hide his delight. 'Put one in his belly.'

'Wait,' Meckets boomed. 'There'll be no shooting. Judge is on his way. This is a condemned man and we're going to hand him over.'

'You mean we've rode all the way up here just to give him up to the judge?' Harlan stared contemptuously at Tillman. 'No point in waiting so far as I can see. End result is the same.'

Whipple kicked Tillman's gun so it skidded across the yard.

'Still claiming you're innocent?' Harlan sneered.

'I never shot June,' Tillman said quietly.

'Just like you never shot my pappy,' Whipple said. 'I've been waiting for this day, I can tell you.'

'That was never intended,' Tillman said wearily. 'You know that. You know how sorry I am.' He looked straight at Whipple.

'Sorry ain't worth a damn,' Whipple said. 'An eye for an eye is what Pappy would have said.'

Irritated by having to listen to Whipple go over old ground, Meckets butted in. He ordered Tillman to sit on the porch beside the reverend, where Harlan could keep an eye on them, and told Perez to go inside the cabin and rustle up some coffee. He announced to them all that, as they were in for a long wait, they might as well quit yabbering and conserve their strength.

For a while no one spoke. Harlan brought a chair out of the cabin, sat with his .45 in his lap and faced Tillman; Whipple found an old packing case and settled down beside him; Meckets occupied the old porch rocker. Eventually Perez appeared with a coffee pot in his hand.

'Not them,' Whipple said when Perez poured tin cups of hot black coffee for the prisoners.

'Leave him be.' Meckets overruled him.

Not out of concern for him and Bullhorn, Tillman reckoned. Meckets just wanted to keep Whipple in his place. Tillman turned to Perez and made a point of thanking him for the coffee.

'Ride out to the ridge, look out for a sign of the judge's posse,' Meckets told Perez. Then we might know how long we've got to sit here.'

'OK, boss,' Perez nodded.

He retrieved his old plainsman's hat from where it had ended up and walked over to his horse. Meckets raised a hand in thanks as Perez mounted up.

'You thought about what I was saying?' Bullhorn turned to Meckets.

'I thought about it,' Meckets said.

Bullhorn's right eye was swollen like a plum; dried blood matted his moustache.

'Most times, I believe people,' Bullhorn went on. 'Because mostly they tell the truth.'

'What's he talking about?' Harlan snapped.

'He reckons June could have rode south that night,' Meckets said. 'Reckons Tillman didn't meet her at the ford.'

'What?' Harlan glared at him. 'I thought this was all over. I thought Tillman was found guilty and sentenced to hang.'

'Tillman says he didn't do it,' Bullhorn persisted. 'I believe him.'

Harlan laughed. 'Who cares what you believe? You're a snake oil salesman.'

'In my experience,' Bullhorn said firmly, 'most times people say what they believe is the truth.'

Harlan appealed to Meckets. 'Hear this? What's he trying to say?'

'I'm saying,' Bullhorn declared, 'that the judge got it wrong. You all did.'

'Hell with you.' Knocking his chair backwards, Harlan jumped up as if he'd been stung. He thumbed the hammer and waved his gun in Bullhorn's face.

On his feet a second later, Whipple grabbed his gun out of its holster.

'You two hotheads sit back down,' Meckets bellowed. 'The judge will be here soon enough.'

' 'Course, my theory about everyone telling the truth don't always work,' Bullhorn added. He stared first at Harlan then fixed his gaze on Whipple.

'Which one of you two fearless young cowboys shot Lilly?' Bullhorn kept his gaze steady.

'That was self-defence.' Harlan's eyes slid over to Meckets for support.

'She took a shot at us.' Whipple backed him up but he sounded uncertain.

'We didn't know it was a woman,' Harlan added quickly. 'How could we?'

'Took a shot at you?' Bullhorn's voice was steel.

'Well, she . . .' Whipple swallowed his words. 'It was self-defence, anyhow.'

'Lilly never missed,' Bullhorn said. 'If she took a shot, then one of you wouldn't be here now.'

'Who cares?' Harlan said. 'She's dead. She came for us and I plugged her.'

'You said it was self-defence.' Bullhorn's voice was barely a whisper. Anger drained the blood from his face. 'There were two shots. That's right, ain't it?' He looked at Meckets.'

'I heard two.' Meckets stared at him. ' 'Course. . . .'

'Two shots.' Bullhorn looked at each of them in turn so there was no mistake.

He levered himself to his feet.

'I'm fetching Lilly's gun.'

'Hell you are!' Harlan jumped up again.

'Ain't going to use it.' Bullhorn turned to Meckets. 'You've got my word.'

'This is bull,' Harlan said. 'What are you trying to prove?'

'Sit down, both of you,' Meckets said.

He got to his feet, reached across and pulled Harlan's gun out of his hand. He flicked open the chamber and held it up for them all to see.

'Two slugs missing.' Meckets shrugged. 'So what? Still could have fired in self-defence, couldn't he?'

He thrust the gun back in Harlan's hand.

'You believe that?' Bullhorn said.

'That's what he said.' Meckets sat down again.

'I taught Ida and Lilly to shoot,' Bullhorn said. 'Broke up the journey from town to town. We'd buy a box of slugs whenever we came to a general store and when we pitched camp that night we'd loose off at a whole line of tin cans off a tree branch. Throw 'em up into the air sometimes, see how many times we could knock 'em sideways before

127

they hit the ground. The girls got mighty good at it, especially Lilly. Both of 'em turned out better shots than me. They used to laugh about that.'

Bullhorn stared at the ground for a moment. 'If Lilly took a shot at something, she never missed.'

He looked across to where Harlan and Whipple sat. Both of them avoided his eye.

'He can brag about how good a shot she was all he wants.' Harlan looked at Meckets. 'She rode right at us. She was wearing man's clothes. She was angry. Like I said, it was self-defence.'

The heat of the day was in the air now. The men felt the warmth of the sun on their faces, and the dry air in their throats tasted of dust. Meckets leaned back in the rocker and for a moment it looked as if he was going to close his eyes. Harlan and Whipple, anxious for him to believe them, waited for him to speak. Bullhorn leaned his head back against the cabin wall; the purple swelling over his eye ballooned beneath the skin. Tillman stared out into the junipers. From where they perched, the pair of redstarts fluttered to likely foliage, fanned their wings across the leaves and gleaned the startled insects, whose movements gave them away. Then they hopped back to their original perches, beaks crammed.

'Angry?' Bullhorn said.

'She was,' Harlan insisted.

'Rode right at us,' Whipple echoed.

'She rode down there to see what was going on,' Bullhorn said. 'That's all.'

'Well . . .' Harlan looked to Whipple for support.

Bullhorn knew the more matter of fact he sounded, the more it needled Harlan.

'Can't see what might have made her angry. Never seen

128

her angry and I've knowed her a long time.'

'That's bull,' Harlan snapped. 'Everyone gets angry.'

Bullhorn shrugged.

'I'm just saying,' he said, 'if she was angry, what do you reckon caused that?'

'The wagon,' Whipple blurted. 'She saw the wagon was burning.'

Bullhorn's reassuring voice confused him. He glanced at Harlan, unsure whether he had said too much.

'And you did that?' Bullhorn said softly. 'Burned out the wagon?'

Whipple hesitated. He looked at Harlan again.

'What are you gonna do about it?' Harlan snapped. 'I told you you ain't welcome here last time.'

Whipple grinned, pleased he hadn't said the wrong thing after all.

'You shouldn't have done that.' Bullhorn's voice was still quiet but his tone had changed.

Whipple looked nervous. Harlan laughed.

'Did you shoot June that night?' Meckets said suddenly.

'What?' Harlan looked as if someone had knocked the wind out of him.

'You heard me.' The steel in Meckets's voice meant his question had to be answered. 'If the reverend is right, she rode out to the herd to face you down. It's the kind of thing she would have done, ain't it?'

They waited for Harlan's reply.

'Everyone who knew her would agree with that,' Tillman added.

'You're taking the say-so of some snake-oil salesman over me?' Harlan glared at Meckets, his voice tight with fury.

'He ain't got nothing to gain from this,' Meckets said.

'Hell he ain't!' Harlan yelled. 'He rode down here, didn't he? Rode down thinking he could save his friend from the rope?'

'Ain't the same,' Tillman said. 'You know that.'

Harlan stood and faced them like a boxer backed against the ropes, shoulders dropped, stooped slightly forward, hands balled into fists. His face was pale and his eyes darted between Meckets and the men sitting on the porch boards as if he was afraid one of them was going to make a move on him.

'Where's the proof?' Harlan spat. 'June was found in the ford. That ain't nowhere near the herd. It's where he gunned her down.' He turned to Tillman. 'Murdered his own wife. The judge said so.'

'Sheriff guaranteed there was no sign of a struggle at the ford,' Meckets said.

'He shot her face to face—' Harlan persisted.

'There weren't no tracks of anyone following her out from the ranch, neither,' Meckets went on.

'That's right.' Harlan laughed. 'You can't accuse me of nothing.'

'You shot her down by the herd.' It was a weighty accusation. Meckets heaved himself to his feet as though he needed to gather his strength to make it. 'There ain't no tracks because you rode up the stream and dumped her body in the ford where Tillman found her. Two shots to the chest, just like that girl in there.'

'This is bull.' Harlan shifted his weight from foot to foot as if he was treading on live coals. 'You're making this up. You ain't got no proof.'

'Makes sense though, don't it?' Bullhorn added quietly. 'June rode down and accused you of cutting the herd to your face and you shot her. Meckets is right, she confronted

130

you and you shot her for it, just like you shot Lilly.'

'Hell with you all.' Harlan choked on his words; he didn't know which way to turn.

Whipple scrambled to his feet and backed away as if he was afraid that Harlan might lash out.

'I'll make sure I tell the judge when he gets here,' Bullhorn said. 'He ain't going to want to hang an innocent man. And what's he going to do when he learns you shot Lilly?'

Before Bullhorn finished speaking, Harlan's .45 was in his hand. His face was tight and bloodless; his eyes blazed.

'No one won't tell the judge nothing,' he yelled.

He pumped two shots into Bullhorn's chest. The reverend's eyes were wide with surprise; blood exploded down the front of his shirt and he slumped forward.

'And you.' Harlan turned his gun on Meckets. 'You took the word of this two bit preacher instead of me.'

Two more shots. Meckets didn't have time to speak; he didn't have time go for the gun in his belt. His body toppled out of the chair and crashed down on to the porch.

Harlan snatched Meckets's gun and pointed it at Tillman.

'Only reason I ain't putting a slug in you is there's a price on your head. You're already a dead man. When the judge gets here I'll tell him you shot these two while you were trying to escape. You ain't got no one to speak up for you now.'

12

As Bullhorn's dead weight toppled against him Tillman struggled to get at Harlan. Sitting on the floor of the porch with his back to the cabin wall, it was impossible to jack himself up fast enough. Harlan sidestepped Tillman's grab for his legs and watched him sprawl face down in the dirt.

Tillman heard the *snick* as Harlan thumbed back the hammer on his Colt. He heard him yell something. A second later he heard a whiplash crack and felt the side of his head detonate as Harlan boot-heeled a vicious kick. Instinctively, he covered his head with his arms to shield himself from the storm that followed.

Gunpowder flashes burst inside Tillman's skull. Harlan's voice screamed in his ear but he couldn't make out the words. Blood and dirt clogged his mouth. When the kicking stopped, someone hauled him backwards by his legs and heaved him up into a sitting position. The back of his skull banged against the cabin wall; a steel spike drove into his brain; blood in his eyes blinded him.

'That's enough. That's enough.' It was Whipple's voice. 'If you knock his head off, we won't be able to claim no reward.'

As Tillman wiped away the blood sunlight stabbed his eyes and his vision swam. Harlan and Whipple stared down at him. Tillman raised his arms to shield himself in case the kicking began again.

'How much longer before the damn judge gets here?' Harlan barked. His anger seethed: he needed an outlet for it.

'Won't be too long.' Whipple tried to calm him down. Knowing how Harlan's temper flared, he sounded jittery.

'We've got to keep it cool,' Whipple said. 'Or the judge ain't going to believe us.'

'What are you talking about?' Harlan rounded on him.

'I'm just saying: if we're all riled up when he gets here, he's gonna reckon it was us caused this mess.'

'You'd jump at your own shadow,' Harlan sneered. 'No way anyone will blame us for anything. Tillman is a wanted man. He's sentenced to hang. He grabbed a gun and shot Meckets and the reverend because they were going to turn him in. We overpowered him. No way the judge is going to believe a convicted murderer over us.'

Whipple righted one of the chairs, took it a few paces out into the yard and sat down opposite Tillman. He drew his Colt and laid it in his lap.

'Thought about this day for a long time,' Whipple announced. 'The day I finally get justice for my pa.'

'Where the hell is Perez?' Harlan ignored him. 'He should have seen something by now.'

Tillman's head swam. He couldn't concentrate on what the two of them were saying. Not that their words mattered. If he closed his eyes he could tell them apart by the tone of their voices: Harlan's horsewhip sneer, Whipple's bootlicking whine. A stampede thundered through his head; he ran his tongue round the inside of his mouth to

133

check which of his teeth were loose; the taste of blood and dirt made him heave. He tried to assemble his drifting thoughts, but the effort was too much.

Images floated into Tillman's head almost as if he were dreaming. First, he was on the ranch house porch, standing in front of Bullhorn in his Sunday jacket and brand-new Stetson. June was beside him in a white dress, holding a posy of jewel flowers. Meckets stood the other side of her in his best shirt and a bootlace tie. Everyone was smiling.

He heard Bullhorn say 'I now pronounce you . . .'

When he turned he could see the row of ranch hands in clean shirts and polished boots, awkwardly holding their hats in their hands. They were smiling too. And when he kissed the bride, their whoops bounced off the sky.

Then there was another image. It was dark. There was the sound of water running over stones. The front of his shirt was wet; he stumbled because his knees were suddenly weak. He was holding June's cold body. Her eyes were closed; the way her head lolled back frightened him; her soaking clothes clung to her. The dark stain on her shirt front told him she was dead.

'Hey.' Harlan's voice pulled him back into consciousness. 'Stay with us, Tillman, we want you wide awake when they put the noose round your neck.'

A drum banged inside Tillman's head. He tasted blood again.

'Won't have long to wait now,' Harlan jeered. 'Rider coming.'

Tillman pulled himself up against the cabin wall. Harlan stood a few feet away, looking straight at him. Whipple was on the far side of the yard staring in the direction of the ridge. Someone had laid out Meckets's and Bullhorn's bodies on the porch. Their arms were stiff by their sides, their legs were straight and their eyes were closed. The dark patches on their shirts showed how they died.

'Ain't the judge,' Whipple called. 'There's only one of 'em.'

'It'll be Perez,' Harlan said. 'Tell us how long the Governor will be.'

'Give me a drink of water,' Tillman said.

He couldn't distinguish between the thumping in his head and the sound of the hoofbeats. His shoulders were stiff; his whole body burned with pain.

Harlan fetched a canteen and slung it down beside him. Tillman had never tasted anything so sweet as the water he poured down his throat.

'Things turning out pretty nice, ain't they?' Whipple sauntered across the yard. 'With a noose around Tillman's neck, I get payback for my pa; you get him in the frame for June.'

'You don't know nothing.' Harlan turned on him. 'What are you crowing about?'

'And we both get the reward money.' Whipple grinned. 'I'm just saying, things are turning out pretty nice.'

'You're a real rooster, ain't you?' Harlan's eyes narrowed. 'If you'd wanted payback for your pa, you'd have gone after Tillman years ago.'

Whipple froze; his face fell.

'And that reward money is mine,' Harlan said. 'I tracked Tillman up here. You just came along for the ride.'

'I'm owed,' Whipple said quietly. 'Tillman shot my pa. I never had no payback till now.'

Harlan laughed. 'Your pa was a thief and a drunk. He had it coming; all the guys said so. And when the accident happened, what did my uncle do? He took pity on you. You were taken in and looked after. He treated you like his own son.'

Harlan stared at Whipple. His snarky words flicked like a whip; he wanted them to hurt.

'Number of times I've heard you bleating about payback this, payback that; I'm gonna get Tillman for what he done to my pa; I'm just waiting for the right time, I'm picking my moment. It's all bull. You never mean to do nothing.'

Harlan turned and walked away a couple of paces as if he couldn't be bothered with him any more. Bright-red spots appeared on Whipple's cheeks; his shoulders dropped; he stared at the dirt in front of his boots; the shadow from the brim of his hat fell across his eyes.

'I'll kill him now,' he said.

He drew his gun and pointed it unsteadily at Tillman.

Harlan spun round, his gun was already in his hand.

'Pull that trigger and I'll scatter your brains across this yard.'

Whipple glanced at him. Harlan crouched low; his aim was rock steady.

'Put your gun down,' Tillman said softly. 'He means it.'

'Hear that?' Harlan sneered. 'Tillman wants me to get my reward.'

'Put it down,' Tillman insisted.

As Whipple hesitated Harlan snicked back the hammer on his .45. There was a pause while Whipple made up his mind.

'OK,' Whipple breathed.

He slid the gun back into its holster.

'That's better,' Harlan said. 'Now we can carry on like before.'

Whipple didn't look at him.

'You'll get your payback,' Harlan assured him. 'You can watch while they tie the noose.'

'And watch you get away with murder,' Whipple said.

Harlan stood up.

'Keep your mouth shut. I didn't hear you complain when you took your cut for the hundred head we took through Stealer's. I didn't hear you complain about that this season or last.'

'That's different,' Whipple said. He spoke quietly so as not to antagonize; he knew how quick Harlan's temper was. 'That ain't killing.'

'Tell that to the judge. They hang rustlers in this territory. You know that just as well as I do.'

'Still . . .' Whipple persisted. 'June—'

'What do you know about that?' Harlan rounded on him. 'You weren't even there. Anyhow, it was dark; I thought it was Tillman. I knew he was tracking us. The guys said he'd been asking questions. How was I to know who it was?'

'You're saying shooting June was an accident?' Whipple's voice was quiet again, as though he couldn't believe what he heard himself ask. 'How could you mistake her for Tillman, even in the dark?'

Harlan had an explanation ready but the words jumbled in his mouth and he couldn't get them out. He hadn't expected to be talking about this. Whipple saw him hesitate and believed he was lying. He turned away.

'It's the truth,' Harlan insisted. 'Tillman had been asking questions; any of the guys will tell you. We were down by Stealer's when a rider came out of the shadows. I was sure it was Tillman. Headed straight for me, ignored all of the others. That's how I knew.'

Harlan waited for Whipple to agree with him; he expected back up because Whipple always backed him up.

'It wasn't my fault,' Harlan added. He wanted Whipple to be convinced.

'Never is your fault,' Whipple said. Thinking about June's death hurt him; physical pain twisted inside him. Hearing Harlan say it was an accident made it worse; he despised him for it. Usually Harlan intimidated him but now he didn't care. 'Always someone else's. You blame me because Meckets let me live in the ranch house; you blamed that girl for asking what the hell you were doing when you set light to the wagon; you blamed that travelling preacher because he asked questions; you blamed Meckets because he made Tillman stock detective.'

'Shut up,' Harlan snarled. 'Right now.'

The sound of hoofbeats just the other side of the ridge caused them both to turn.

'Hear that?' Harlan said. 'That's your payback coming. That's judge and jury for your pa. That's what you've always wanted, right?'

Whipple heard something in Harlan's voice which he had never heard before. Harlan was asking him to agree with him, pleading with him almost. Not demanding or threatening; not bullying or blackmailing like he always did. Harlan needed him to be on his side. Whipple knew that meant Harlan was afraid.

After the tragedy, as far as Meckets was concerned pairing his nephew with Frank Whipple's boy was the obvious thing to do. As far as he knew the two of them worked well together. Harlan was more experienced: Whipple could learn from him. *Be like Harlan*, Meckets

138

told him; *Harlan will teach you about the herd; Harlan will show you how to do things.*

Whipple put up with being ordered about and pushed around; Harlan was the boss's nephew and that was the way it was. After Meckets took Whipple in to live in the ranch house, Harlan told Whipple he was the lucky one; no one had ever done him a favour like that. Because of it, Harlan made him feel indebted and Harlan could call in the debt any time he liked. When they argued Whipple never found the strength to win; when they fought, Harlan always pinned him down.

When Harlan suggested cutting the herd he told Whipple that ranch hands always did this: here, back in Texas, everywhere. It was normal. No one would take any notice; no one would even know. Whipple went along as usual, just like Harlan knew he would. When Harlan handed out his cut, he took it.

But right now Harlan was asking him for something. Whipple studied him. Harlan should have been wearing some sort of smile, but his face was pale and drawn. He should have been pleased: hoofbeats meant the judge's posse was on its way. Instead, there was a look in his eyes which said *don't let me down now.* Maybe Harlan figured he had gone too far this time, Whipple reflected, even for him. For the first time, Whipple sensed he might have the upper hand.

'Hey, Whipple,' Tillman pulled himself upright. 'You gonna do the right thing or are you gonna let him tow you along like always?'

Whipple rounded on him. 'You got some nerve, speaking to me like that.'

'I'm asking—' Tillman continued.

'Never speak to me like that.' Whipple cut him short.

'This is my payback for what you did. You shot my pa and now I'm gonna see you hang. That's how this is going to be squared off. Don't think you can weasel round me. Don't think anything else is going to happen, because it ain't.'

'Hear that, Tillman?' Harlan crowed. 'Me and him is partners, our word against yours. When the judge gets here you ain't got a prayer.'

A rider appeared over the ridge. He stopped for a minute and waved to them. It was Perez. As he made his way down the slope towards the cabin, they lost sight of him behind the junipers for a moment. At the sound of his horse the redstarts, frightened, flew up into the air; their feathers flashed like drops of blood.

As Perez rode into the yard his eyes took everything in. The two bodies laid out at the far end of the porch, Tillman leaning back against the cabin wall with blood on his face, Harlan and Whipple standing in the yard, waiting for him to speak.

'What kept you?' Harlan said.

Perez couldn't take his eyes off the bodies. He stayed rooted in his saddle as if he didn't want to risk climbing down.

'What happened here?' He naturally turned to Tillman.

Tillman's look explained everything.

'Well?' Harlan insisted.

'Posse's on its way,' Perez said. 'They got a couple of others with them. Stayed up there to try to figure out who it was, but I ain't never seen them before.'

'What do they look like?' Harlan was edgy.

'Dunno.' Perez shrugged. His eyes slid back to the bodies. 'Just guys.'

'Judge with them?' Harlan said.

Perez nodded.

'Six of 'em, riding like they ain't got time to lose.'

'Look like a hanging posse?' Harlan wanted to be sure.

Perez stared at Tillman's swollen, broken face. He took in the way his shirt was ripped from being dragged along the ground and noticed the way he nursed his ribs.

'It's a hanging posse,' he said. 'Couldn't be nothing else.'

13

Within an hour the posse stormed into the yard. Judge Duval was out front, his face carved out of stone. His black jacket and hat were coated in trail dust and the collar of his dirt-stained shirt was held in place by a single gold stud. Riding alongside him, Ida led Ludza's horse by the reins. Ludza, with his hands tied, clung to his saddle. Three square-built guys whom Tillman recognized from the courtroom made up the posse.

The judge dismounted and waved away Harlan's greeting.

'Fetch the rope and find a branch.' His tone was gravel in a bucket. 'You know what we came here to do.'

One of the guys from the posse swung himself down off his horse, untied a lasso and held it ready. Ida hauled a terrified Ludza out of his saddle, dragged him over to the nearest porch post and lashed him to it. Once the judge dismounted, he noticed the bodies.

'Tell me what's been going on here.' He squinted at Harlan.

'We captured the prisoner,' Harlan said. 'Held him for you because we didn't want to take justice into our own hands.' He paused to give the judge a chance to thank him, or at least acknowledge that he had done the right thing. 'He broke free from us, grabbed a gun and shot these two men—'

'Your honour. . . .' Tillman was on his feet. 'That ain't what happened. If you'll let me speak—'

'Quiet. You're a convicted murderer and an escaped prisoner.' The judge didn't turn to look at him. 'If I want you to open your mouth, I'll let you know.'

Suddenly realizing that Bullhorn was one of the bodies lined up on the porch, Ida ran across the yard. She dropped to her knees beside the reverend and stared into his beaten, lifeless face.

The judge carried on trying to make up his mind about Harlan.

'You're saying Tillman shot both of them?'

'That's right, sir. Then we overpowered him.'

'Your honour . . .' Tillman interrupted. The judge ignored him.

'Including this Bullhorn character?' The judge stared at Harlan.

'That's right, sir,' Harlan's voice was earnest and sincere.

'Why would he do that, exactly?' The judge spoke slowly, so there could be no mistake.

'He was trying to escape,' Harlan looked confused, as if he couldn't figure why the judge didn't understand.

'You got proof of this?'

'I got a witness,' Harlan said confidently. A smirk lifted the corners of his mouth. He had guessed this was what the judge would ask him and he was prepared. He indicated Whipple.

'That's right, your honour,' Whipple said. 'Tillman shot these two and then we overpowered him.'

'Who are you?' The judge glared at him.

Whipple explained.

'You're saying this was deliberate murder?'

'Yes.' Whipple sounded less sure.

'You saw him pull the trigger?'

'Yes.' Under the judge's stare, Whipple's confidence drained.

'Your honour,' Tillman tried again. 'If I could . . .'

'Quiet,' the judge barked. 'No need for you to speak. I know you're going to tell me you didn't do it.'

He stared at Whipple.

'This young woman told me that she rode down here with the reverend to speak up for Tillman. The reverend thought he was an honest man. Explain to me why Tillman would shoot him.'

Whipple hesitated; Harlan jumped in.

'Blazed away, sir. Got hold of a gun and nobody was safe. He's a desperate man. It was all me and Whipple could do to hold him down.'

'What about you?' The governor turned to Perez.

'I didn't see nothing,' Perez said. 'They sent me up on the ridge to keep watch. When I got back the shooting was over.'

'That's right,' Harlan chipped in. 'He didn't see nothing.'

The judge scowled. 'One thing that makes for a sound judgment is a reliable witness,' he declared. 'When Tillman was on trial for shooting his wife I had Meckets, ranch owner, father of the girl, long time friend of the accused and an intelligent man. On top of that, I served with him in the war. He pointed the finger at Tillman. That was good enough for me. On top of that, Tillman admitted being in the right place at the right time and admitted there had been a falling out between himself and the victim.'

With his hands clasped behind his back, the judge started to pace. His eyes were screwed up in concentration and his mouth a hard line as he thought aloud.

'This time, what have I got? The word of a convicted murderer against the word of two ranch hands. They might back each other up but they can't produce a shred of evidence.'

The judge stopped abruptly and looked into the faces of each of them in turn. Ida got up from beside Bullhorn's body, wiped her eyes and waited for him to go on.

'I can see why Tillman would want to shoot Meckets. But not Bullhorn. All these fellas can tell me is that he was "blazing away". I've heard some damn stupid stories in my courtroom but this one don't even make sense.'

'That's right,' Tillman chimed in. 'Both of them are lying.'

The judge ignored him.

'If you've got reason to trust a man and he tells you something, there's a good chance it's the truth. If you ain't got reason to trust him, chances are it ain't.'

Tillman pushed himself to his feet. His bruised face twisted into a smile.

'That's right, your honour. There ain't no reason to trust these two.'

The judge's posse closed in on Harlan and Whipple. None of them had drawn a gun yet, but their hands were ready over their holsters. Whipple's face crumpled; Harlan's was the colour of snow. Harlan tried to say something but the words collapsed in his mouth.

'Doubt we'll ever get to the bottom of it,' the judge reflected. 'But seems to me it ain't likely Tillman did this.

If he didn't, that only leaves you two. You said yourselves the Mexican was up on the ridge.'

'Now, sir, that would be jumping to conclusions.' Harlan's voice shook.

The posse took steps closer, ready to grab him.

'Me and Whipple have told you the truth, sir.'

'That's another thing,' the judge added. 'When someone you can't rely on swears they're telling the truth, they usually ain't.'

Harlan struggled to stop himself saying anything else: his words made a choking noise in his throat.

'So, I'm free to go?' Tillman's heart skipped. A smile twisted through the bruises on his face. At last someone believed him. There was justice after all.

The judge felt for a tin of Bull Durham in his jacket pocket and slipped a plug into the side of his mouth.

'Can't believe I heard you say that, Tillman.' The judge looked surprised. 'Soon as the guys find a strong enough branch, we're going to hang you.'

Tillman rushed forward but the posse rounded on him. Two of them grabbed him and wrestled his arms behind his back while the third man, who held the coil of rope, scanned the junipers.

'You've just said . . .' Tillman began.

'Just because I don't trust these two water snakes don't mean you ain't guilty,' the judge roared. 'You shot your wife. I convicted you in my own courtroom on the testimony of a reliable witness, a man who was formerly your friend and partner.'

'Listen to me . . .' Tillman caught his breath.

He tried to wrench himself free, but the judge's men twisted his arms until his shoulders burst and the pain knocked the air out of him.

146

'On top of that, you broke out of jail the night before you were due to hang. Might even have killed a guard, but I ain't got any evidence that says so.'

'I got a witness.' Tillman's voice was hollow. The pain in his arms made his breathing weak. 'A reliable man, someone you ain't got no reason to doubt.'

The judge croaked a laugh.

'My experience, a condemned man will say anything to save himself.'

At the edge of the junipers one of the guys from the posse found a suitable branch, slung the rope over it and pulled hard to test its strength. Although the man was heavier set than Tillman, the branch held.

'Tie his hands behind him,' the judge ordered. 'Set him on a horse.'

'Listen to me.' Tillman fought for breath as the men lashed his wrists behind his back. 'I didn't kill her. I can prove it.'

'Too late.' The judge's voice was lead. 'You're a convicted man.'

'Bullhorn was reliable.' It was Ida's voice.

Everyone turned towards her. She stood beside Bullhorn's body, her pale face stained with tears.

'He rode down here to speak up for Tillman. He wasn't at the trial.'

The judge hesitated.

'No reason to doubt what you say, ma'am. And I'm aware he would have spoke for Tillman at the trial. That wouldn't have stopped Meckets's testimony though, would it? Would have been one against one. No disrespect, but I reckon I still would have come down on Meckets's side.' He turned to the guys waiting to lift Tillman on to the horse. 'Let's get on with this.'

Over by the junipers the guy tested the branch again.

'What about my witness?' Tillman's words clawed in his throat

The two men heaved him into the saddle.

'Ask Perez where he got that hat,' Tillman called.

'Get it over with,' the judge barked.

One of the men led the horse over to where the noose hung from the juniper branch. The other followed to hold Tillman in the saddle if he tried to break for it.

'I found it.' Perez stepped forward from the porch. 'Why?'

'Where?'

'Dunno. Down by the herd someplace. Why?'

The horse halted below the juniper. The judge's man lashed one end of the rope to the trunk.

'That's my old plainsman,' Tillman said. 'You've seen me wearing it. You've seen June wearing it.'

Perez looked confused.

'You're saying I stole it?'

'What is this nonsense?' the judge bellowed. 'You're about to meet your maker and all you can worry about is somebody stealing your damn hat?' He nodded to the man under the tree. 'Put the noose on him.'

'Perez is my witness,' Tillman shouted. He twisted in the saddle to avoid the noose.

'I've seen him wearing it.' Ida spoke up. 'Last time we were down here, I remember now. His wife bought him a new hat for the wedding. He said he was going to throw it out and she said she'd wear it when she was riding.'

'That's right,' Tillman said.

'Don't mean a thing.' The judge spat a stream of tobacco juice. 'Put the noose on him.'

'When did you find it, Perez?' Tillman was desperate.

148

'Which day?'

With Tillman twisting every which way in the saddle, the judge's men couldn't reach up to get the noose over his head from the ground. One of them marched back across the yard, mounted up and rode back alongside him.

'Think, Perez. Which day?'

The men held Tillman still for long enough to slip the noose over his head and tighten the knot around his neck.

Perez walked out into the yard.

'The night the boss's girl was killed. I came back from the herd to look for Harlan. We were supposed to be moving the beeves south. But he wasn't there. I saw this old hat caught on a creosote bush.'

'She was wearing it,' Tillman's voice was hoarse. 'She tucked her hair up under it. When I found her in the ford, she wasn't wearing a hat. That's evidence she rode south that night to confront Harlan, just like I said.'

'Hang him,' the judge roared.

The horse sprang away. Tillman's body lurched at the end of the rope; his legs kicked wildly.

'He's right,' Ida screamed.

She dashed across the yard, barged between the judge's men, flung her arms round Tillman's legs and held him up.

'He's telling you, his wife rode down to the herd that night. Don't you see?'

Tillman's weight was too much for her. Her knees buckled. Perez ran to help her.

'Someone shot her down by the herd,' Ida yelled. 'Moved her body up to the ford to where they knew Tillman would find her. When he brought her to the ranch it looked like he'd done it.'

Perez grabbed Tillman round the knees and hoisted

him until the rope was slack. Above him, Tillman's body swayed, the noose cut into his neck and his breathing came in gasps.

'That's a lie,' Harlan backed away across the yard. 'Don't listen to her. She don't know nothing.'

Chalk-faced, Whipple backed away with him.

The judge's men hurled themselves at Perez and felled him like a tree. He let go of Tillman's legs and pulled the men away from Tillman's swinging body, down on top of him. As the men picked themselves up, Ida ran at them. She cannoned them off balance for long enough for Perez to scramble to his feet, grab Tillman's legs again and heave him shoulder high.

'He's innocent,' Ida screamed. 'We've given you the proof.'

Horrified by the sight of Perez holding up the hanged man, the judge hesitated. His mind raced. If this story about the hat was true. . . ? There had been no signs of a struggle at the ford. If someone had ridden up the steam from the herd, there would have been no hoof prints. . . . If the woman had been shot down by the herd, her body could have been carried up and left for Tillman to find.

Almost before the judge realized, Harlan had crept out of the yard, round behind the cabin to where the horses were tethered; Whipple was with him. Another second, they would be mounted up and away.

One of the judge's men landed a massive punch on the side of Perez's jaw. His knees swayed, his feet staggered but he still managed to hold Tillman up. He buried his face in Tillman's legs to shield his face from the second swing he knew would come.

'Cut him down,' the judge yelled suddenly. 'Let no one say I ever hung an innocent man.'

It took a minute for the men from the posse to struggle with the knot from at the trunk of the juniper. The rope snaked over the branch and Tillman's body crashed to the ground. His face was swollen out of shape, his cheeks flamed purple while his lips and a disc of skin round his mouth were ash white; rope burns scarred his throat. Perez lifted his head off the ground; Ida clawed at the noose enough to loosen it. Tillman's eyes were closed but they heard breath scour his windpipe. He was alive.

14

As the deputies set off after Harlan and Whipple Ida fetched a scoop of water from the barrel inside the cabin door and held it to Tillman's lips. Beside him, in the dirt, the rope curled like a shed snakeskin. When he opened his eyes Ida's and Perez's concerned faces swam into his vision. They helped him up and supported him to the old rocker on the porch.

'Unorthodox procedure,' the judge reflected. 'I guess I just overturned the verdict of one of my own trials.'

Tillman lay back in the chair and let Ida minister sips of water to him. His throat was too painful for him to speak.

'I trusted Meckets,' the judge continued. 'He served under me in the war, Lee's Army of Northern Virginia. We were together at Sharpsburg. He was a brave soldier and an honourable man. Felt sorry for him for the loss of his daughter. Guess his grief made him turn on you. He wouldn't be the first to react like that.'

Looking straight out into the junipers, the judge told a story of how he caught a bullet in the thigh at Miller's cornfield just as the enemy mounted a charge. Meckets ran back into the field of fire, he said, heaved him across his shoulders and ran with him to safety.

152

'Owe him my life,' the judge said simply.

He allowed himself a glance across to where Meckets's body was laid out beside the reverend. Then he tore his eyes away, stared into the trees again and concentrated on the redstarts in the high branches.

Tillman ran the tips of his fingers carefully along the rope cuts round his throat. The torn skin was the outer sign of damage. Every breath cauterized his swollen windpipe; internal bruising constricted every gulp of air. Sometimes he was on the verge of blacking out.

Eventually, the judge turned to him.

'Made a mistake,' he said gruffly. 'Passing judgment on you like I did. You're an innocent man and I almost caused you to hang. To my knowledge, it ain't never happened before. I'll make damn sure it don't happen again.'

Tillman studied the judge's face. There was honesty there, conviction that what he was doing was right. The judge looked at him straight.

'I'm sorry.'

Later, Ida asked about the death of her friend. She had seen Lilly's body when she first entered the cabin but held back her questions until she was strong enough. Perez told her how she had ridden straight up to Harlan when she saw him setting light to the wagon. She yelled at him, Perez said, demanded to know what the hell Harlan thought he was doing. She didn't draw on him; she gave him the chance to explain. Harlan's answer was to shoot her on sight.

The judge listened to all this.

'You a first-hand witness?' he asked. 'Prepared to swear this was what you saw?'

Perez said he was. The judge got abruptly to his feet

and marched across the yard to where the track led down to the ford. He rounded the side of the cabin in search of a view over the valley that would allow him to check the progress of his deputies.

Ida stayed beside Tillman while the heat of the day passed; she cradled his head in the crook of her arm and offered the scoop of water whenever he needed it. Together they watched the redstarts in the branches of the junipers.

'Later on, maybe you can help me find a quiet spot where we can lay Lilly and the reverend to rest.'

When Tillman signalled that he wanted to write, Ida fetched one of his drawings and a pencil from inside the cabin.

I know a place, he wrote on the back.

Ida took a bundle of twenties from her jacket pocket.

'Almost forgot this. Ludza had it on him.'

She handed the money to Tillman but he pushed it away.

Pay for the wagon, he wrote. *How did you get it back?*

They turned to look at Ludza, who was still tied to the porch post where Ida left him. He sat with his head bowed, knees drawn up under his chin and tried not to be noticed.

'Hey, Ludza,' Ida called. 'Tell 'em how come I got the money.'

'I just . . .' Ludza squirmed awkwardly. 'She asked me, your honour.' He caught the judge's eye. 'I handed it straight over. I ain't all bad.'

'Really?' As the judge stomped back across the yard he curled his lip.

'Asked him if he wanted to kiss me.' Ida laughed. 'Told him he'd have to move in real close. Then I stuck a .45 in his gut while I pulled the money out of his pocket.'

Ludza hung his head.

The deputies took longer than everyone expected. The judge reported seeing dust clouds to the north. Harlan and Whipple had given their pursuers the slip and beaten a path into the desert.

'Headed across country,' the judge said. 'If they'd stuck to the trail, my boys would have 'em back here by now.'

The afternoon heat settled on the yard. The judge paced; Tillman lay still, trying to recover his strength; Perez drew water for the horses; Ludza avoided catching anybody's eye. Ida went inside, coaxed a fire in the cabin grate and made coffee. She watched as Tillman blew on his and saw him wince when the liquid burned his throat. The judge found a chair in the cabin and brought it out on to the porch. He beckoned Perez over.

'Been thinking,' the judge said. 'When we ride out I'd like you to come with us. You're an honourable man. I could use someone like you.'

Wholly unused to being the centre of attention, let alone receiving a compliment, Perez hardly knew where to look.

'Deputy's pay ain't great but it's an honest line of work,' the judge went on. 'You'd like the other guys. We're a kinda team.'

He was surprised that Perez didn't immediately jump at the offer. Then he saw what Tillman had scribbled on the paper.

I need you here.

Perez began to mumble embarrassed thanks.

'All right, all right.' The judge was two steps ahead of him. He held up his hand in mock surrender. 'I see what's going on.' He turned to Tillman. 'You'll be taking over the ranch and making him foreman.'

Tillman scrawled one word.

Partner.

He held the paper up.

'Partner in the ranch?' Perez looked shocked.

Can't do it on my own, Tillman wrote. *Just think about it.*

'Don't have to,' Perez said. A sunshine grin lit up his face.

'What about you?' the judge turned to Ida.

Stay on the ranch with us, Tillman scrawled.

'If you're thinking of offering me a job as a cook, think again.' Ida laughed. 'I don't fancy playing kitchen maid to a ranch full of saddle-sore cowpokes.'

Don't have to cook.

Tillman grinned at her over the top of the paper he held up.

'How do you expect me to spend my time? Cowboying?' She laughed again.

Why not? Tillman wrote.

'I've had some offers in my time,' Ida said. 'Can't say this is one of the more attractive. I'll stay with you until I've seen to the buryin'. I'll take your three hundred, get the wagon repaired and head up to Phoenix. I've got a sister there. She'll let me stay for a while.'

Tillman shrugged.

Sorry, he wrote.

The judge was anxious to be on his way. He strode up and down the length of the yard and then went out to see if he could catch sight of the deputies again. Perez began to talk about the ranch. He had ideas about how they could divert the stream, irrigate more land and increase grazing; he talked about fencing the entrance to Stealer's

Creek and posting trustworthy men down there to see off any rustlers.

'We should build a new bunkhouse,' he went on. 'The guys are cramped where they are; they're always complaining. Part of the walls are rotten anyway.'

Pull it down, Tillman wrote. *They can stay in the ranch house.*

Perez's lit up as he watched Tillman's hand scrawl out the words.

'They'd reckon they'd made their jack if you let 'em do that.' Perez laughed. 'Some of them have lived in bunkhouses all their lives.'

Tillman leaned back in the rocker and listened to Perez's schemes for improving the ranch. Perez had cowboyed for years. He'd been on round-ups, cattle drives, ridden in rodeos, spent lonely nights guarding the herd against rustlers and months on end living in the saddle. No one had ever asked him for his opinions on how a ranch should be run. Now was his chance. Ideas flooded out of him.

'Sounds like you're gonna have one helluva place,' Ida said.

Change your mind, Tillman wrote and pushed the paper across to her.

They sat under the shade of the porch for two more hours until they heard the hoofbeats of the deputies' horses. Heat from the afternoon sun hammered the yard, warmed the shadows between the junipers and toasted the air inside the cabin. Still with his hands tied, Ludza rested his forehead against the porch post and closed his eyes.

Two deputies rode into the yard ahead of Harlan and Whipple; one followed behind. The prisoners' arms were lashed to their sides. Their faces were tense and drawn.

The judge was waiting for them.

'Heard evidence against you,' the judge announced. He nodded towards Perez. 'Got an eyewitness says you shot that girl who rode with the reverend. Before you say anything, just know that he's a man I can rely on. You're guilty of shooting June Tillman and putting her husband in the frame. You killed Meckets and the reverend. I'm taking you to the jailhouse. You can wait there till you stand trial.'

Neither Harlan or Whipple spoke. Harlan glanced briefly at Tillman, noted the rope burns on his neck and looked away; Whipple stared at the ground.

'As for you,' the judge turned to where Ludza crouched on the porch, 'I'm handing you over to the prison governor. He can deal with you.'

While one of the deputies heaved Ludza on to a horse the judge announced they would be heading out right away. He strode over to the porch, touched the brim of his hat to Ida, shook Perez's hand, then Tillman's. As he climbed into his saddle, Tillman pushed himself to his feet to watch the horses wheel out of the yard. Ida and Perez stood beside him.

'More than a day's ride back to the jail,' the judge called down to them. 'Should make it by sundown tomorrow if we leave right off. Guess we'll have to stop somewhere to catch a few hours shut-eye, but I ain't inclined to rest until these no-goods are behind bars. Besides that, I got unfinished business at the jail. There's a line of cattle thieves and murderers waiting on me up there.'

The judge was granite-faced. 'Know what the jailbirds call it, whenever my posse rides up there?'

Tillman didn't smile. The rope burns hurt his neck;

158

swelling tightened his throat. He couldn't manage anything louder than a whisper.

'Hanging Day,' he said.